INSIDE OUT *360*

Lati`a D. Johnson

I0629883

JOHNSON PUBLICATIONS

Newtown Square PA 19073

Cover Copyright © 2011 by Johnson Publications all rights reserved
Cover layout/design Designs by Sheshe
Cover Photo by Doss Tidwell
Model: Tammy Fay
Editor: Carla M. Dean, U Can Mark My Word

Copyright © 2011 by Lati`a D Johnson
All rights reserved. No part of this book shall be reproduced or transmitted
in any form or by any means without prior written permission of the author
and publisher.
This book is a work of fiction. Names, characters, places and incidents
either are products of the author's imagination or are used fictitiously. Any
resemblance to actual events or locales or persons, living or deceased, is
entirely coincidental.
ISBN:9780615441016
Published by:
Johnson Publications
Newtown Square PA 19073
Printed in the United States of America

Contact for comments or to order book
www.johnsonpublications.biz www.myspace.com/insideoutbook

Dedications

This book is dedicated to everyone that has ever loved and supported my dreams. You all are truly my inspiration. Thanks for taking this ride with me.

I LOVE YOU!

Thank You

I thank God for all of my gifts that I possess. Nothing is possible without him.

INSIDE OUT 360

INTRODUCTION

The streets were lined with beautiful trees. Hues of yellow and powder blue surrounded each branch, while the sweet smell of floral essence floated through the air and made it known that spring was quickly approaching. The streets were busy with cars going to and fro in Philadelphia's posh neighborhood of Balla Cynwood, the home of the city's ballers, top officials, and few well-known street pharmacists. The tall buildings surrounding the area were the workplaces of some of the most influential doctors and lawyers.

Tiff pulled up to the front of a twenty-story plush building. After checking herself in the rearview mirror, she proceeded to exit her car. She turned around to set the alarm on her latest toy, a sea-blue Benz convertible. Cars slowed down as she strutted across the parking lot dressed in a one-piece strapless denim jumper and 4inch studded Marc Jacob stilettos. Her hair was a flowing mane of layers, and her Chanel shades were perfect for her small face. Tiff was on a mission, and even though she felt like crap, she definitely didn't look like it. She lived by her motto: Never let 'em see you sweat.

Tiff was on her way to her standing appointment with Dr. Deborah Hawkins that took place every other week since six weeks ago. She was feeling bad on so many levels. She and Evea hadn't been in touch with each other in years, and the love of her life's death anniversary was slowly approaching.

Tiff stepped off of the elevator and was greeted by Dr. Hawkins' secretary who always was pleasant and made her feel comfortable.

"Good morning, Ms. Dease. I'm glad to see you made it in," the secretary said with a smile.

Tiff gave a half smile in return and replied, "Yeah, I almost turned around at least five times on my way over here."

"Well, you know Dr. Hawkins would have hunted you down."

Both ladies laughed at the thought of Dr. Hawkins running in her good heels to catch Tiff. As the ladies finished their good laugh, the doctor appeared in her doorway to usher Tiff into her office.

Dr. Hawkins stood 5'7" tall, with natural curly shoulder-length hair and milk chocolate skin.

"Hello, Ms. Tiffany. I'm glad to see you smiling these days."

Tiff replied, "Not for long."

The office was decorated in calm colors of cream and sea-foam green. Dr. Hawkins directed her to lie down on her comfortable chaise that sat in the left corner of the room in front of the window. Tiff obliged, and as she lay staring at the ceiling, tears began to stream down her face at the thought of re-living that horrible night when her love was taken from her. Tiff blamed Evea for everything.

Rapid thoughts raced through her mind as she talked to herself. "Evea, why did you have to be so selfish? Now I lost you and Lex."

Dr. Hawkins plucked some tissues from the box nearby, handed them to Tiff, and then asked,

"Tiffany, why are you crying?"

Tiff just sobbed even more. Gently, the doctor explained that if she was not ready to face that night, they could reschedule the hypnosis session.

Sniffling, Tiff replied, "Doc, I'm ready to put this behind me, so let's do this."

Dr. Hawkins began relaxing Tiff and asking her a series of questions to take her back to where all of her pain began.

Tiff grabbed hold of the pillow and ushered Dr. Hawkins into her world...

Tiff arrived at the show and was searching for Lex. While she was looking the opposite way, Lex crept up behind her dressed in white linen. Lex grabbed her waist and said, "Damn, ma, you sexy as shit. Are you waiting for someone?" He loved to creep up on her; that was his style.

Tiff poked her ass out and replied, "I think I just found him!"

They both laughed.

Tiff was falling harder than she thought, which made her task even harder to complete. Tiff loved fucking Lex, and she was determined to follow through with the first half of her plan. Tiff self-parked in the parking lot to make sure she would be able to taste that dick once more. Tiff told Lex that she left something in her car and needed his assistance walking back to get it. Lex found it odd that Tiff did not use valet parking, but he followed her anyway.

While Tiff was on her way to get her last shot, Naih and Noah arrived at the party wearing all-white denim. They sat a few rows back from Té and Evea. Naih was nervous, but she was packing heat, so she had protection. She was trying to figure out how she would get away to get to Pier 11 before Noah, who could not wait to give her what he thought she deserved.

Once Tiff and Lex made it to the car, Tiff bent over pretending to look for her purse. That's when Lex saw that she had no panties on.

"Damn, ma, you got a nigga on brick!"

Lex's hormones rode hard like wild stallions. Tiff forgot she had her gun on her right thigh. Lex saw how the black holster and gun rested on her toned thigh. This made him more aroused. Knowing this turned him on, she hiked her ass up more and made sure she had a perfect arch in her back. Lex moved closer to Tiff and put his fingers in her wet ocean. She was so wet that her pussy talked back to him like it had vocal cords. Tiff climbed in the car and spread her legs open as she invited Lex for dinner. Diving in headfirst, Lex licked her from front to back until the seats were drenched with lust.

The security guard allowed Adam through. It was intermission, and the fashion show was over. The music was about to begin as Adam slowly moved through the crowd, excusing himself to the hundreds of people in the walkway. The

Spring Fling show was packed due to the big names on the lineup. Beyoncé, Jay-Z, TI, Lil Wayne, and Chris Brown were just a few of the scheduled performances. Adam was almost past the stage and could see a clear walkway.

Lex and Tiff had just arrived at the seating area. They had thoroughly enjoyed themselves in the car, and Tiff was glowing brighter than the jewels on the stage. While trying to get to their seats, they laughed about their brief episode. Looking around, Lex noticed a tall, curly head nigga fighting to get through the crowd ahead of him. That can't be Adam, *he thought to himself, but when Adam turned sideways to let someone get past, it was confirmed. Lex had to follow him and finish what he had started. He thought quickly about what he was going to say to Tiff to get away.*

After they made it to their seats, Lex stood up and told Tiff, "Yo, ma, I'll be back. I just saw one of my homies. I'm gonna go holla at him."

Tiff looked at him and noticed he had begun to sweat. She said to herself, Okay, homie my ass. *Still, she would let Lex go handle his business.*

The lights started flashing, and TI hit the stage. When the music to "What You Know About That" *sounded over the speakers, the crowd went wild. Té told Evea that he was going to the bathroom. Noah got up and began to move when he saw Té get up. Naih had left about ten minutes prior to the show starting. She told Noah she had to go to the restroom. However, she was on her way to meet Zayne at the pier.*

Adam got through the crowd and made it to Pier 11, but no

one was there. He stood there looking at his watch, anticipating another brief moment with his love. Corn and the rest of the crew were in the building right above the pier with their weapons drawn and pointed at the center of the pier. Zayne and Naih were in position behind two old dumpsters like two children playing a game of hide and seek. They could not wait to see Noah so Zayne could make his move.

As Adam turned around and looked at the water, reminiscing about Evea and their last time together, Lex quickly appeared with his gun drawn. Adam heard heavier footsteps than those of a female, and at that moment, he realized he had been set up. He spun around with his gun drawn, and both men stood there with their guns pointed at each other. Adam was confused; he did not know Lex and did not know what he wanted with him.

Standing there with a chrome Desert Eagle pointed in his face, Adam asked, "Who the fuck are you?"

"Nigga, I'm your worst nightmare!" Lex replied. "I should have finished you off in your car. This time, I won't miss!"

"Pussy, you're the one that shot my baby," Adam said, while looking Lex straight in the eye.

Just then, Lex let off a shot that hit Adam so hard he stumbled backward. Adam returned fire, hitting Lex in the stomach. Corn and the boys witnessed the shit going down, but Corn told them to hold their fire because Lex was down there. Corn did not know how Lex knew Adam, and he could not make out what they were saying to each other.

Zayne emerged from behind the huge dumpster, walked up behind Adam, and shouted, "You dirty nigga, drop the fucking gun!"

Naih ran from under the overpass, yelling, "Wait! That's not Noah!"

She startled them and shots rang out. Naih fell to the ground, her blood turning the cement a deep burgundy hue. Adam was shot in the chest, but he managed to run for cover as bullets flew from everywhere. He made it a few feet away, then collapsed on his stomach. Te` and Noah arrived just in time. They walked up, letting bullets rain down like spring showers. Zayne managed to maneuver his way behind a cement boulder.

The last conversation he had with Evea ran through Adam's mind, as he accepted that he might not make it through the shootout alive. Zayne was on wild-out mode. He didn't give a fuck. His love had been shot and was possibly dead. He was out to revenge his homie's death.

Lex was hurt, alone, and had several niggas shooting at him. He saw visions of the many faces of the niggas that he killed throughout his years of being the crew's enforcer. He did not know how Té and Noah were involved with the situation, but he did not care. The only thing on his mind was surviving. So, he busted shots at them, too.

Growing worried, Tiff went to go look for Lex. She got a few blocks away from the show and heard shots. She quickly removed her gun from her holster. Cautiously approaching the scene, she saw Lex being shot at, but she could not see who was shooting. Tiff wanted to walk away and let the niggas shooting at him do her dirty work. Lex stood up to return gunfire and was shot several times in the torso. He fell to the ground, gasping for air.

Tiff stopped dead in her tracks. "NOOOOOOOO!" she screamed, while running up and dumping back. She hit Zayne in the head, and he fell to the ground lifeless. At that moment, she knew she was in too deep to just walk away.

Té was still after blood! As Adam's motionless body lay on the ground, Té could not express in words the rage he felt for him. Instead, he allowed his gat to speak for him. Té stood over Adam's still body and reloaded his clip. When Té's clip locked into place, though, Adam rolled over with bloodstained eyes piercing through Té and let his gun ring like a four-alarm fire alert.

"Your wife was a great fuck, but now, I'm gonna fuck you up!" His words were harsh and reeked of rage and detest.

Tiff crawled low and pulled Lex to safety. Her lover, who just a few hours ago she had planned to murder, was now her priority. She struggled with mixed emotions. She held him in her arms, and he spoke words they had never spoken to each other before.

"Ma, I'm not going to make it. I can feel it."

Tiff begged him not to say that.

"Listen, I'm fucked up bad, ma. I love you...I loved you from the first day we..." Lex's breath evaporated like steam from a boiling teapot.

On her knees, Tiff wept. For the first time, she had found love. Yet, she couldn't even keep it. She kneeled there with sounds of bullets echoing in the background as her heart turned to stone.

Her tears covered Lex, but they were not enough to save him. His lifeless body lay in her arms, while bullets and bodies surrounded Tiff. She struggled to process everything that had just taken place. Tiff continued to weep uncontrollably over Lex's corpse, as she gathered her gun, some of Lex's personal belongings, and anything else she deemed important. Then, with a slow lurch, she headed back toward the show.

She was fucked up over the shit that had just gone down, but she was still a wise gangstress. She knew the police would soon be arriving on the scene, and she needed to be far away. While walking the few blocks back, she replayed in her head what she had witnessed and been involved in, wondering how she would go on. One block from the show, she tried to pull herself together before she saw Evea. However, Tiff was startled by the abrupt appearance of Evea, who was on her way to see what was taking Té so long in the bathroom. Tiff looked as if she had seen a ghost floating in mid air. Evea did not say a word; her face had a vocabulary of its own.

Tiff stood there with Té's bloody shirt in one hand and Lex's chain, car keys, and gun in the other. Evea approached Tiff with caution and took the gun out of her right hand. That's when Tiff fell to the ground, taking Evea with her as she let out cries that sounded like screeching wild animals in *pain. Evea wrapped her up in her arms, matching Tiff's screams. Deep beneath their consoling embrace festered turmoil and hatred.*

Chapter 1

"Yo, where that cash at, nigga?"

"I told you I would have it later on today."

"You said that shit two days ago!"

The angry gunman pulled out his nine millimeter cocked it back, and let off a round. Noah dodged and ran, while giving the gunman some of his own hot shit back. Noah's luck ran out, though, and the last thing he saw was the smoke from the barrel.

"Keep the change, nigga!"

Bang! Bang! Bang! The knocking on the door woke Noah up from his nightmare. He jumped out of bed sweating and breathing like he had just run ten miles straight.

"Who is it?" he yelled, angrier that he had just got murked

in his dream than at the fact someone's knocking had awakened him.

"It's me, Corn, nigga. What's taking ya ass so long?"

Noah made it to the door and swung it open when he heard the familiar voice on the other side. Corn entered the house and walked slowly down the Italian marble floor of Noah's long hallway. The pictures on the wall were fine art fresh out of the art gallery.

"Why you not ready?" Corn questioned Noah. "We was supposed to meet the fellas at the spot thirty minutes ago."

"Man, I was having this crazy-ass dream. I had to lay a nigga down in this one."

Corn laughed. "Nigga, how you sweating and breathing all hard? It looks like a nigga laid *your* ass down in your dream."

Noah just looked at Corn, hating the fact that he was right. "I'll be ready in a minute. Call the crew and let them know we on our way.

"Cool," Corn replied. "Just hurry up, man. This shit never happened when Té was here."

"Nigga, please."

Noah ran upstairs to shower and get fresh for their business meeting. Since Té was gone, Noah had been running shit, and he was quickly finding out that being the head nigga in charge was harder than he thought. Noah emerged from his bedroom suite looking duggy. His curly, dark black dreads were lying perfectly in place, and his shape up was tight. He had on black denim Cavelli jeans and a jeweled Ed Hardy t-shirt. Noah was toting his accessory that matched everything, a nickel-plated 9mm equipped with silencer. He was ready for whatever.

Noah hurried down the stairs so Corn would not become any more restless than usual. "My nigga, what's the deal?" Noah yelled, letting Corn know he was ready to go.

Corn held up his right index finger to signal Noah to be quiet while he finished up his call.

"Damn, nigga, who you speaking to that's so important I got to get the church finger?"

Corn shot back, "Now you worried about the wrong shit, my nig."

They both gave each other some dap and headed out the door. Corn and Noah walked down the wide, long driveway trying to decide which hot ride they would take, one of Noah's or Corn's brand-new, dope-boy-slick, black Range Rover. They jumped in Corn's ride and proceeded to their destination. During the ride over to the west Philly spot, they discussed crew shit and the latest territory they were trying to take over.

Corn loved Noah like a brother, but it was obvious he was no Té. Noah was wild and at times reckless in his business decisions. That was one of the reasons Té had kept him as the sniper. He was ready to let off whenever. Noah gambled too much and did plenty of fucking, which was always his weakness. He was part of the reason the girl Naih had been able to infiltrate and try to set Té and the crew up at the shootout.

When they arrived at the spot, the block was jumping. Feens were everywhere, and the little homies were serving heavy. That was a sign of great business and profits to come. As Noah and Corn hopped out of the Range and proceeded to walk up the block, bitches stopped and waved, while creaming in their panties at the sight of fresh money and power. The sun was shining bright, and everyone was buzzing about the upcoming spring fling in the city. The small overcrowded street was filled with row houses, but every other structure was boarded up.

Corn and Noah said what's up to the homies as they walked through the cluster of people like celebrities. Reaching their destination, they noticed the street soldiers on the porch were on point and loaded with heavy firepower. They each gave dap as they approached the front door of the army-green painted house. They did the special knock to be sure the boys inside didn't let off shots when they opened the door. As they entered the spot, various greetings were spoken from all around the room.

Jay-Roc was at the table ready for the business meeting. Love was on his cell phone boo-lovin' with his latest booty call, which is how he got his name in the first place, and G was sitting on the brown leather sofa playing Madden. Noah's eyes canvassed the room and stopped dead on the newcomer. When G turned around, Noah looked as if he had seen a ghost.

"What's up, my nigga! When did you get home?"

Noah was extremely happy to see one of the old crewmembers finally out of the pen. G had done some hard time for Té back in the day and was just hitting the streets.

"I just touched down last night, nigga. I see you still the

same old Noah Just a little older than I remember.

Both men embraced as they shared a mutual laugh about Noah's habit of going against the grain.

By this time, Love had hung up the phone and chimed in, "Nigga, that's why we had the meeting with such short notice. It was supposed to be a surprise, but instead, you surprised us by taking all damn day, fake-ass pretty boy. You ain't even light skinned."

They all roared in laughter.

"Alright, that's enough of that!" Noah yelled out, appearing to become serious.

Jay-Roc yelled out, "Go to hell!"

The men slowly got themselves together and made their way to the table. Noah took Té's seat at the head of the table. It still felt funny to be sitting in his deceased cousin's spot. Noah and Té were very close, and he took his death harder than any one of them. He felt even more fucked up that day because looking at G was like looking at Té. They were always told they looked alike when they were growing up. G stood about 6'3" and was light brown, with dark, wavy hair and a full rich beard. The only thing that separated Té and G was the hair on G's head.

The meeting got underway with

Corn informing the boys the block was doing wonderful bringing in approximately fifty thousand dollars every few days per house. All the fellas yelled and cheered for the success of their empire, while G just sat there thinking, *Damn, my homies are really eating, and I'm about to get a piece of the pie, too.*

Anxious to discuss the most anticipated topic of the hour, G interrupted the buzz. "Yo, I know we celebrating me coming home and our shit bombing, but I need to know something. Did that nigga Adam get touched yet for offing my big homie Té?" The mention of his name choked G up and brought him to rage all at the same time.

Noah replied, "The nigga done went into hiding for some years since that shit went down. Nobody has seen him, and I mean *nobody*."

"What happened to Evea?"

"She been missing, too. Kayla is with Evea's mother, and nobody really knows where that is. Evea was real fucked up after Té's death."

G just sat there staring into space. Kayla was his goddaughter, and he had missed so much of her life. Now his one true friend was gone, and he may never see Kayla again.

"Kayla has to be about fifteen or sixteen years old now, right?"

Noah counted the years on his fingers, then looked up and said, "Yeah, that's about right."

G excused himself from the table and went outside for some air. The fellas resumed their meeting without commenting on G's obvious mood.

"Okay, next order of business is G's coming home party. Did you book the usual place, and is everything ready?" Corn asked.

"Yes, sir," Jay-Roc replied. "Everything is in place, and

I'm ready for some 'get right' tonight!"

Noah sat back in the chair and looked around the room as if expecting five-o to rush in any minute. "We need to wrap this shit up. What's going on with the new spot we're opening?"

Love replied, "I'm on that right now. I was just talking to my connect when you came in. She put me on to this little town in upstate Pennsylvania that don't have nobody else supplying all of the rich white folks wit' that pure nose candy."

Noah got a little more comfortable in his chair as Love continued. "If everything works out, we will be making double what we making at the other houses weekly."

"Damn!" everyone said at once like a church choir.

Love went on. "Me and Honey gonna rent a place as a couple using fake names and take over the 'burbs…Mr. and Mrs. Snowman."

"That sounds good," Noah responded, "but I don't know this chic. How you know she clean?"

"'Cause I know. Trust me, she won't be involved in any day-to-day operations."

Noah's phone rang, breaking up the party. "Yo, talk to me, sexy."

"Hey, baby, where you at?" a sultry voice said through the phone.

"I'm finishing up with the boys. Why? What's good?"

"That good dick is what's good, and me sliding down on it!"

"Damn, shawty, you got a nigga on brick. Hold on."

"We know. Meeting over," Corn said, already knowing what was up.

They all rose from the table while cracking up in laughter.

Jay yelled, "That must be, Ms. Boss Bitch!"

Noah fanned him away with his hand, then returned his attention back to the phone conversation. "Shawty, I'm on my way."

Noah rushed out of the door, gave all the fellas some dap, and then said to G, "It's good to have you home," as he headed for the Range. Corn knew what was up, so he didn't even ask. Corn just threw him the keys and told Noah that he would meet up with him later at the party.

Noah turned around and yelled back, "Be sure to take care of G!"

G laughed and looked at Corn. "Still the same old Noah...slave to the pussy."

Corn replied, "I'll say 'Yes, master' to some good pussy any day!"

Noah hit the expressway like a bat out of hell. He was ready to experience all his shawty had to give. He could not control the erection he got just thinking about her. How sexy she was and the shit she did to him was something out of a book or movie. He was ready to be taken to the edge and hung off the cliff. Noah loved all the things that got his adrenaline going, like great sex, money, and gambling--all in that order.

Noah hit full speed ahead, and put Corn's system to use, blasting Plies all the way home as he nodded his head and sang along with each verse. He could see the house in his view and was growing more excited as he took the exit off the expressway. Noah pulled up to the huge driveway and noticed his shawty's car was already there, which could mean only one thing. She was inside preparing for their encounter. He approached the double mahogany wood doors and placed his key in the lock. Upon entering the stylish, well-furnished home, he could smell the scent of vanilla and cinnamon. Then he laid eyes on her, and it was all worth it.

Their eyes met in the dimly lit living room. Shades of chocolate brown and burgundy filled the room, and the flickering of candles gave the room a subtle glow. There she lay on an oversized loveseat draped in a sheer thong and jeweled heels that exposed her entire foot. Next to the loveseat was a tray with various toppings, consisting of strawberries, chocolate syrup, caramel syrup, Cool Whip, and her favorite frozen peaches.

No words were exchanged as she stood up and guided Noah toward the chair that she had situated in the center of the room. She took his tongue in her mouth and played with it, applying just enough pressure. Noah moaned from her touch. Then she slid down to her knees and opened his pants with her teeth to unleash his python. She undressed him nice and slow while he rubbed and pulled on her perky nipples. Once she had him in full glory, she poured chocolate syrup on his pleasure rod as she inhaled every inch of him. Noah squirmed in the chair and moaned as though he was a wounded animal. One treat after another adorned his shaft, and each treat she put on him, she completely cleaned off with her mouth. When

Noah's body began to shake, she knew what that meant, but he wasn't ready for the party to end.

Noah gathered enough breath to say, "Shawty, let me taste you." He picked her up and faced her head toward the top of the loveseat. Grabbing a frozen peach slice, he began inserting it into her opening. He pushed in and out as she screamed in ecstasy. Next, he held the peach slice on her clit and moved it slowly in circles. The coldness sent chills up her spine.

"Oh shit, I cumin'!" she yelled repeatedly before exploding.

Once she couldn't cum anymore, he laid her sideways, spread her legs far apart, and mounted her. His rod slid in with precision. "Mmmm," she whispered as he hit each spot inside of her. She rotated her hips in a snakelike motion while he watched her beautiful, round ass jump with each stroke.

In her sexiest voice, she proclaimed, "Daddy, I love how you feel inside of me," and before she could say anything else, they both were singing in unison.

"Oh...oh...oh, TIFFFF!!! Dis pussy is so wet!"

In a fit of orgasms, Noah fell on top of Tiff, and Tiff's body shook uncontrollably. No other words were spoken. They both fell asleep comfortable in each other's love juices.

*****

Across town, Corn was preparing things for G's welcome home celebration. He made sure he had enough cash lined up to get G a nice wardrobe and a fly whip, compliments of all the homies chipping in some stacks. G had always been a part of the squad, and he put in plenty of work before getting booked for a petty drug charge that got him sent up for some years. Corn called G to be sure he was ready to go.

"What up, my nig?"

Corn yelled through the phone.

"Hello. Who's this?"

"I'm sorry, Mrs. Reynolds. I was calling to speak with G. Is he there?" Corn felt stupid addressing G's mother like that. While waiting for G to come to the phone, he whispered to himself, "Dis nigga need a phone, too."

G made it to the phone gasping for air.

"Yo, Corn, where you at?"

"I'm outside, man. Come on. We got stuff to handle. You got me talking all crazy to your mom. Hurry up, man!"

"I'm on my way out. One."

G stepped outside and canvassed the area for Corn before spotting him in a canary yellow Spider at the top of the block. His eyes grew with excitement as he approached the vehicle. He hopped in, and as usual, they greeted with a handshake and kept it moving. Corn and G said nothing as they blazed up the highway headed for a baller's dream, the King of Prussia Mall. G adjusted his seat for comfort, and they both nodded their head to classic Biggie Smalls' *Life after Death* CD all the way to their destination.

When they pulled up in the parking lot, all eyes were on them. Even the sophisticated, stuck-up women stopped in their tracks. They wanted to see who would step out of one of the most expensive cars on the streets. Corn whipped into a free parking space, and at the flick of a switch, both butterfly doors opened. He stepped out wearing a honey, crushed linen, two-piece pants set and camel skin loafers that played well off of his golden skin. G was no slouch either. He wore a fitted black tee with dark denim Red Monkey jeans and a pair of black on red throwback #3 Jordans. He was equipped with that fresh prison glow and a body that looked as if he was chiseled by an artist…all two hundred and forty pounds of him.

The men approached the massive chrome double doors at the mall's entrance and proceeded to glide in. First stop was the Louis Vuitton store. G and Corn equipped themselves with watches, shoes, and other fly accessories. Next stop was Bloomingdale's, where they purchased G's everyday wear that included denim, designer underwear, and polo shirts.

G was definitely happy to be home and even happier that he had niggas that were real in the game. Corn and G laughed as they exchanged stories about Té and their smutty episodes. Corn stopped in the center of the mall to take a phone call. While he was on the phone, G spotted a new store that looked to contain some gear that was just his taste. He waved at Corn to get his attention.

Corn approached G as he hung up his phone." What up, dude?"

"You see that hot shit in the window? What store is that?"

"Oh shit, I almost skipped that one. That's Gees 2 Gents. I get all my exclusive shit from there. Let's go check it out."

The two men entered the store, and G went wild buying all

that he could. As they were in the corner picking out custom shirts and hats, they realized they were under surveillance. Corn looked up and their eyes met. Cindy stood 5'5" and was half black and Korean. She had hair that resembled 100% silk and two full breasts the color of coffee and cream, which sat up on display within the fabric of her black suit jacket. Corn could do nothing but smile.

"Damn, I forgot she worked this shift," Corn remarked to G, who was still looking down at the shirts.

G looked up just in time. "Damn, who dat?"

"That's Cindy," Corn replied, "but I call her Candy because her ass is sweet like sugar."

"Do Candy got a sister named Cake? 'Cause a nigga definitely tryna bake something tonight."

Corn gave him dap and cracked a half smile. Cindy whispered in her co-worker's ear and then gestured for Corn to come over to the counter. Before G could finish talking, Corn had disappeared. Cindy escorted him to the back of the store without saying a word. Once in the back, it was as if they were both animals.

Cindy slammed Corn against the wall where racks of designer clothes hung. He reached up to grab hold of the shelf above him in order to brace himself for what was in store. Cindy stood before Corn with her black Armani suit now crumbled at her feet. She wore nothing but black lace thongs with the diamond string, a black lace pushup bra, and 3-inch black Kenneth Cole stilettos. She began to pleasure herself as Corn just stood there looking in amazement at her beautiful body. *Flawless,* he thought to himself.

She slid Corn's pants down to his ankles and his boxer briefs went with them. Cindy squatted low to the floor with her legs spread wide and played with her clit slow and hard. She moaned and shook each time her soft fingers stroked up, and she pulled on the ring that hung from her clitoris. By now, Corn's rod was hard as cement. He began stroking it and rubbing it gently on her lips. Cindy parted her lips, and his rock hard extension filled every inch of her mouth. She moved her soft pink tongue round and round on the tip as she sucked with such force that the sound echoed off the small storage room walls. Her body trembled, and she made sensual hissing sounds with a mouth full of flesh. Corn pounded her face like he was in the pussy. She took every inch of him as it tickled the back of her throat. Cindy rode her own finger while slurping on Corn harder and harder. Her nipples got so hard, they tingled without any touching. Tugging at her clit piercing, she brought herself to a climax and the juices ran down both legs. Cindy's jaws tightened up as she came back to back. This was a chain reaction; Corn's body gyrated like he was a wild horse bucking. Roaring one swift AWWWW, his soldiers marched down Cindy's throat. Drained, Corn wiped his stick off and pulled up his trousers.

"Call me later so we can finish what we stared," Cindy whispered with a smile, then disappeared into the employee bathroom.

Corn emerged from the back and was greeted by a smiling G, who had more bags than they could carry.

Corn smiled back and said, "Now let's get your ass a BlackBerry for all the numbers you gonna get at your party."

Then he and G disappeared into the mall's atmosphere.

Chapter 2

Positioned comfortably in her oversized cream recliner, Evea sat in front of her six-foot picture window admiring the view. She found that spot in her room to be relaxing and comforting whenever she wanted to be alone to think. Hues of bright orange, rust, and ivory filled her bedroom. Evea's custom-made bed was raised off of the floor by its own platform. Black and white photos of she and Kayla when her daughter was a baby were displayed throughout the sitting area. As Evea sat there, she could almost feel the spring breeze blowing on her face. She could see the squirrels playing on the huge tree full of mature lilac and white flowers. Evea planned on soaking up every minute of her day doing only what she liked to do. She did not get many days off to just relax, and this day was going to count.

Evea watched as the mailman drove up to the end of her long driveway and placed a bundle of mail inside of the black box. She knew she needed to go retrieve her mail. So, Evea quickly repositioned herself, letting her feet hang to the floor in order to get up out of the cushioned chair easier. Evea's mind raced as she pitter-pattered to her front door, her feet hitting the cool hardwood floors one at a time. After opening the door, she jogged to the mailbox. The clean, crisp, country air blew her curly long hair away from her face. Her newfound living was far from the junior suburbs she came from.

She desperately hoped she would have a letter from her best friend who she had lost touch with so many years prior. She opened the box and paused to look up in the sky, as if to be communicating with God. Evea replayed the reoccurring dream she had at least five times a month where Tiff somehow got in touch with her mother, and then her mother sent her the letter, and her and Tiff were reunited. Evea missed Tiff more than she could verbalize. She felt all alone because Tiff was the only one in the world that truly understood her. Springtime was the hardest for her. She remembered it not as a time for new beginnings, but the time her love was taken from her. Té's death overshadowed every sunny day and flower bloom.

Evea walked to the house slowly. Her dream did not come true, and she had nothing but bills in the mail. Her peaceful day was anything but that. She was startled by the sound of a heavy truck passing her house and making its way up the road.

"Why the hell people got to rent those noisy-ass diesel

moving trucks?" she said aloud, while proceeding to walk back toward the house as the truck disappeared up the road.

Once inside the house, Evea headed straight for the kitchen. She placed her mail on the granite countertop in the center of her custom chef's kitchen. Evea's day off was not what she had planned. She spun around and grabbed the chrome coffeemaker out of the pantry. *Buzzzz!* Her cell phone vibrated against the counter, and she raced to grab it before she missed the call.

"Hello."

"What's up, Sunshine?"

That voice could melt her heart each time she was privileged to hear it.

"Hey, baby, where you at?"

The voice was that of her love stallion and professed soul mate, Adam. He had managed to still be holding on and living the dream he had since he laid eyes on Evea.

Adam replied, "I'm on my way to get with my favorite girl."

"How are you on your way home so soon?" she asked.

"I'm spending the day with you, and it's nothing you can do about it."

"Adam, you don't have to do that. I know you're busy."

"Baby, I'm on my way. Be ready. I got something special planned."

Evea was reluctant but happy that Adam was going to get her out of her gloomy mood. She felt so lucky to have a man that took care of her so well and truly loved her.

Lati`a D. Johnson

Evea gathered her thoughts and replied, "Okay, sexy. I will be ready and looking my best."

"Love you."

Evea hung on to the words that Adam expressed. She had so many thoughts running through her mind. "I'm so glad God gave me someone that can take care of me since my Té was taken from me," she said to herself, then proceeded with her plans to make Adam truly grateful for being with her.

*****

Adam paced himself as he blazed up the expressway trying to make it home to his baby. He still got brick hard when he thought about Evea getting dressed and doing anything that required her to touch her body.

He was coming from meeting with his new connect that would be keeping a line between him and his customers. With Zane gone, he had to start fresh, and he had just landed a huge account through Manny's cousin, Ramir. He was so nervous that he constantly looked out of his windows like he was being chased by the police. The windows of his Dodge Viper fogged up from him breathing heavily.

Adam was sitting on one hundred thousand dollars in the trunk of the car and another million in hot credit cards. Ramir was already earning him money. Adam was pleased with the new set up where he never met with clients. Ramir was the new man and well worth it. Adam had completely removed his hand from the coke game in the squad and only collected

30

money from Ramir bi-weekly. He hooked Ramir up with the original coke supplier so he would not have any contact with them. He was strictly sticking with his card business. That's what he was well versed on. Now, though, Adam was on his way to spend plenty of money on his boo, and to him, she was worth every penny.

*****

After bathing, Evea proceeded to apply oil to every inch of her body, then slipped on her hot pink Victoria's Secret gem thongs with matching bra. Her double D's that resembled the color of honey sat within the bra's cups just right. Evea dressed in her baby doll Chanel fitted tee, denim BCBG mini skirt, and satin open-toe Farigumo sandals. She had let her hair grow to her mid back, and it was full of sassy curls. While standing still and admiring her image in the mirror, the alarm sounded on the front door, alerting her that someone entered the house.

"Sunshine!" Adam yelled up the stairs, and before he could finish, Evea strutted down the stairs. He stood there with his mouth open. "Damn,"

was all he said.

Evea got closer and planted a sexy wet kiss on his lips.

"I want some of that wet-wet," Adam told her.

Evea kissed his cheek and said, "You can get all the water you want later."

Acting as though he didn't hear a word she said, Adam

kissed her from the right side of her neck and worked his way down to the top of her breast. Evea's erect nipples sent tingling sensations down to her love pocket. Adam felt her arch her back and lean in closely. His excitement grew with each touch of their bodies.

Adam reached under Evea's skirt and began to massage her clit. He knew she could not resist making love to him. As he stroked her clit softly, her river flowed like a broken dam. Evea breaths became shorter and deeper, while Adam's pole pressed hard up against her pelvis. His excitement caught up with Evea's. She wrapped her legs around his waist as he lifted her up and placed her back against the stairs. Evea rotated and slammed down on Adam's manhood as if it were the last time they would be together. Adam watched as she took every inch of him inside of her.

"This is what I been waiting for all day, baby. This wet-wet feels like silk."

The more Adam talked, the closer they both got to climaxing. Evea's mind was clear, and she felt butterflies in her stomach as her body tingled all over.

"Damn, daddy, I'm about to explode. Mmmm, this dick is crazy!" Evea yelled, while playing with her nipples until she erupted.

Adam felt the contraction of her tight walls and juices running down his shaft and scrotum. He flowed like a faucet as they held one another close enough to feel each other's soul. Their outing would have to wait.

Chapter 3

Tiff drove up the road as she struggled to multi-task. Her phone was ringing inside her Fendi purse, and she attempted to retrieve it while managing not to crash into the white Chevy truck in front of her.

"Damn, I can't take another minute of this song," she said, finally grabbing her pearl BlackBerry from the bottom of her purse. "Yo, bitch, dis betta be life or death," she yelled into the phone.

The voice on the other end quickly snapped back, "It is, because you're not where you're supposed to be, as usual."

"Peaches, go to hell!"

As Peaches stood in the mall parking lot with a look of

confusion on her face, Tiff sped by her. She could see Tiff's long hair blowing in the wind as the sun glared off her shinny rims. Tiff was on yet another shopping trip that she did not need. She and Peaches were getting ready for the party of the year--G's welcome home party. Peaches had never had the pleasure of meeting G, but she was always down for a good party.

Peaches waited as Tiff lowered her convertible top and locked the car doors. They were cool, but Peaches clearly was not Evea. Tiff missed her best friend and shopping buddy. She thought about how Evea would not be so uptight about her being late. As she approached Peaches, Tiff cracked a half smile, while Peaches looked as if she could smack the shit out of her.

"What the hell did you say before you hung up?"

Tiff leaned back, and in her high-pitched voice, she said, "Bitch, please. You heard me. Now stop tripping. We 'bout to get ready for a soiree that you can only imagine. You know how my man and his boyz do it!"

"Wow! Now you actually calling Noah your man? That's improvement!"

Both women looked up in the air and laughed until Tiff broke the laughter by saying, "Now let's buy this mall out."

Tiff and Peaches entered the mall and headed straight for Bloomingdale's. They walked and engaged in small talk about their jobs and the niggas they were screwing. The mall was lively with couples and children looking like they were all on some sort of mission. Peaches and Tiff were standing at the pretzel stand waiting for their order, when Peaches spotted Corn and some guy coming out of Gees 2 Gents cracking up laughing. Peaches tapped Tiff's shoulder to get her attention.

"Tiff, ain't that Corn right there? And who the hell is he with?"

Tiff looked up when she heard the urgency in her voice. "That's definitely fine-ass Corn, and oh, that's the man of the hour, G."

"You never told me G was looking that good. Damn!"

"Bitch, calm down. All you see is that fresh out of prison glow. That man will tear your prissy ass up."

"I'm signing up for some riding lessons," Peaches replied.

Tiff laughed as she waved at Corn and signaled for him to meet her halfway. He and G approached the two ladies.

"How you two sexy ladies doing?" Corn asked with a big grin.

"We fine, but what the hell you kee-keeing for?"

"Damn, CIA."

G and Peaches just stood there staring at each other, while Corn and Tiff went back and forth with smart comments. The steam in the air was evident. G was amazed by Peaches' girlish beauty. When she smiled, her deep dimples took over her face.

G had to say something. "Hello, pretty girl. I'm G."

Peaches smiled again, and for a minute, she forgot who she was.

"Damn, Peachy, say something!

The man just introduced himself."

"Hey, I'm Peaches," was all she could muster up to say. She was very turned on by G's looks and furthermore his manners as they spoke. G was just as impressed with her body and smile. He had just come home from prison and ready to run up in something that looked like Peaches. It was very obvious that both Peaches and G were interested in exploring their possibilities.

Tiff broke up the awkwardness by telling Corn and G that they would see them later. The two pairs parted ways and went to prepare for the festivities.

Finished with shopping, Peaches and Tiff headed toward the mall exit. Tiff seemed to have her mind elsewhere. Peaches noticed she had become quiet and solemn.

Concerned, Peaches asked, "What's wrong, T?"

"Why you ask that?"

"Because you just switched gears on me from happy-ass Tiff to quiet, sad Tiff."

"I really don't want to talk about it. It's just so much shit."

'Well, let's start from the beginning," Peaches suggested.

Tiff looked at her and was reluctant to share her thoughts. She did not share anything with anyone but Evea. Not even her man knew what she was really all about.

However, she felt it was time to let some of her pain go.

"I started seeing a therapist."

Peaches was surprised and wanted to know more. "I guess

you miss her a lot, don't you? We all do."

"I miss her and Lex like hell, but I can't stop blaming her for everything. I can't believe she would go away with that nigga after what happened to Té and Lex. This shit is making no sense. Now is when I need her the most, and she never even called!"

Peaches stood in the middle of the mall, bags in hand, trying to console a hurting friend who was in tears. She had little to no answers herself. She just knew Evea was gone and shit was not the same for any of the girls.

Peaches sucked up her tears and said, "T, we got to move on. Things will change. They just have to. Now stop crying. Your twenty-dollar mascara is running."

Both ladies shared a hug and a laugh as they prepared to exit the mall.

*****

The night was a warm seventy-five degrees. The line to get inside the club was so long because regular patrons of SALS and those trying to get into the VIP party for G were standing together. The boys had sent out invitations only to cut down on the riff-raff and rival crew shit. As people approached the entrance, a big white bald guy checked for the black and red velvet invites. Everyone with invitations was let in first. G was loved by many and hated by few, so his party was going to be wall-to-wall people, mostly females.

The night went on and the line seemed never-ending. Half-naked females and overly blinged out guys littered the streets of south Philly. Corn, Noah, Jay-Roc, and the other playas were in VIP enjoying the fun while they awaited G's arrival.

Noah, who was positioned at the blackjack table as usual, yelled over to Corn who was standing nearby vibing with one of the partygoers. "You sure G remembers how to get to South Street? That nigga ain't call or nothing."

Corn replied, "Look, I did my job. The nigga is set. He got fresh lay, a new phone, a condo, and a new ride. He a grown-ass man. He will be here when he get here." After Corn's speech, it was evident he was mellow off the Hennessy in his right hand.

One of the girls from around their block came in the door and announced she had just saw G drive up. The moment everyone was waiting for had finally arrived.

G pulled up in a money-green Lincoln Navigator with 24-inch rims, chrome hardware, and chocolate brown leather interior. When he opened his door, the sounds of Plies spilled onto the streets. His music system was so sophisticated that the sound rattled the concrete beneath him. G stepped out of the truck and turned all the females' heads that were in the area. He was laid from head to feet. He wore midnight–blue silk and linen pants, a custom-fitted cream and blue shirt with an iced out skull on it, a pinstriped denim blazer with a hat to match, and cream baby calf leather loafers.

The valet took his keys, and another gentleman that worked for the club escorted him in the establishment. After G entered the club, Tiff and her crew arrived shinning like new money. Peaches, Kiwi, Sassy, and Plummie stepped on the scene, and the men paused. They made their way to the front of the line and handed the oversized bouncer their tickets.

Once G was in the club, he examined the area where half drunken white girls danced with each other and the DJ spun techno and house music. G canvassed the place for a sign of his boys. He started getting worried until a tall black guy with long braids met him at the bar and escorted him to the VIP section.

He approached the area of the club with caution. Two huge Italian security guards, drawn curtains, and a velvet rope was the barrier between G and VIP. One of the bouncers opened the door to what looked like another world, and G's eyes grew wide. All of the boys ran up and gave him dap as he attempted to take it all in. The party planner had created a fantasy adult candy land. All of the women who were working wore outfits made of edible candy over their naked bodies. It was women of all nationalities and sizes in the bunch. Some entertained the crowd by dancing with each other and sucking on long swirly lollipops. There was gambling going on, lap dancing for girls and guys, and the DJ kept the party live with Jay Z's "Roc Boys (And the Winner Is)". G felt like he was in a scene right out of the movie *American Gangster*.

Jay-Roc quickly went to the bar, got G a drink, and took him center stage to play with the entertainment.

The guys stood around G as they laughed and pointed at the expression on his face. The girls sat at the bar chatting and catching up on the latest news. They laughed about the last big celebration they gathered at. Tiff told the story for the hundredth time about how low she got when shots were fired and how mad she was when her six-hundred-dollar shoes were ruined. They giggled as Tiff's facial expressions pulled them in.

"Shit, I'm just waiting for the next big thing to happen," Plummie yelled. "You know where there is hood there is problems!"

Peaches replied, "Then you should have stayed your ass home on Nobb Hill!"

They all laughed and slapped hands. Tiff became quiet, remembering how she and Evea would have banter like that. The other ladies noticed the shift in her mood, and they too became somber.

Kiwi broke the silence. "We all miss her, Tiff, but we have to try to live our life as best we can."

They spoke of Evea as if she were dead. To them, she was. It had been several years since they had seen or heard from her.

The loud music and blaring lights finally brought the ladies back to focus, reminding them that they were at a party.

Tiff moved seductively in her seat. "That's my song," she moaned.

All the ladies were on the dance floor before the intro to R. Kelly's "Snake" was done. On the way to the dance floor, Peaches could see G being led through VIP by a tall, light-skinned, shapely dancer. When their eyes met, she felt a surge between her legs. Then G disappeared into the lap dance room.

Peaches continued her dance while socializing with other partygoers.

Meanwhile, Noah had not gotten up from the gambling table throughout the party. Tiff approached him and gestured for him to come with her. Noah acknowledged Tiff's presence with a wink and a kiss. Tiff knew what that meant; he would not be done anytime soon. Tiff blew a kiss back and turned to walk away, when she was met by screams and chairs being smashed. A tall, caramel brown man was at the door of VIP being beaten by SALS' doormen. The unidentified man yelled for Peaches and threatened to harm anyone she was with. Peaches quickly attempted to hide from the man. Tiff found her in the corner crying.

"Peaches, who the hell is that loony, and why is he looking for you?"

Peaches wiped her tears and replied, "That's my ex, Jhamal, who's obsessed with me. I can't get rid of him."

Tiff being Tiff, she looked down at Peaches' crotch and laughed. "Damn, what you got between your thighs?"

As Peaches explained their crazy relationship to Tiff, G appeared, agitated that the noise and pausing of music disturbed his lap dance. He had overheard parts of Peaches' story as he approached the damsel in distress.

Chapter 4

Ambulance lights flashed, sirens were blaring, and the steam from the rain was rising from off of the street. Evea stood over Tiff's half blood-covered body and yelled her name aloud. Tiff's eyes were open, but there was no response. Evea stood close by as the paramedics lifted the stretcher carrying Tiff into the back of the ambulance, while other EMT's rushed to the scene where bodies lay everywhere. Evea was in shock. She sat on the curb rocking back and forth while holding Té's clothing in her hands. Evea looked up as the paramedic asked her was she all right.

"Evea! Evea!" Adam yelled.

Evea awoke crying and shaking. Adam took her in his

arms and comforted her like he always did when she had those reoccurring nightmares about the night Té was killed.

Still sobbing, Evea yelled, "Adam, I miss her so much! Why hasn't she looked for me if she's still alive?"

Adam just sat in silence, afraid that if he spoke, he would lose his love forever. Adam hated when their day started off with Evea's nightmares. The day would go slow after the morning began. He sat there holding Evea and comforting her with his sweet whispers of reassurance.

Evea was all cried out, but feeling a little better. She was ready to start her day with Adam. She had one more day left on her vacation, and she wanted to enjoy it without the ghost of Tiff and Té hanging over her head. She hated her nightmares and wanted to get rid of them for good, but no matter what therapeutic techniques she used, they would come back every so often.

Evea prepared her bath as she enjoyed the smell of cinnamon French toast that Adam was preparing for her. After submerging in herself in the bubble bath, she did what she always did to ease her mind.

"Hello, Mom. How are you?"

"Hey, baby, I'm happy to hear from you! I'm fine," a comforting voice on the other end reassured her.

"How is my baby, Momma?"

"Your baby is not a baby no more. She's with her new boyfriend at the mall."

Evea paused for a moment. "I was coming to get her today so we could hang out."

44

Evea's mother just listened to her. She knew what the call was really about, and she was worried. Her mother had Kayla ever since Té's death because Adam feared the person that killed Té may come after them. Little did they know, Evea was living with that person day after day.

"New boyfriend?" Evea posed as a question.

"Yes, new boyfriend. Did she know you were coming?"

Evea sat up in the tub. "No, but I thought I would surprise her. When she gets home, tell her to give me a call. Maybe I can get her for dinner."

"Okay, baby, I will," her mother replied. "Take care of yourself."

Evea hung up the phone as she went down memory lane. She reminisced about when Kayla was a little girl and how happy she and Té were as a family. Evea began to think about everything and wondered if living this life with Adam was worth losing all she had.

Adam whipped around their five-star kitchen like he was a pro. He had thoughts of his mother and family. The smell of cinnamon took him back to a time he once loved. Adam was coldhearted and selfish, but underneath all that toughness he was a family-oriented guy. Adam was taken out of his trance when the smoke detector sounded.

"Shit! What the hell have I done?" Adam's star French toast was ruined, and he knew Evea would be done with her makeover soon.

He cursed all the way down the long driveway as he carried the trash to the dumpster. On the way back to the house, he stopped at his truck to retrieve his belongings. Adam knew the credit cards were small enough to hide in a miniature bag, but the money he picked up from Ramir was a different story. From his dinner meeting with Ramir, two hundred and fifty thousand dollars was hidden in the floor compartment of Adam's chrome gray Denali truck. Adam never let Evea know just how much money he was worth. She didn't even know the extent of his criminal behavior. Evea was not stupid, though. She knew Adam was not a choirboy, but little did she know, he was her worst nightmare! Adam opened up legit businesses, a chain of restaurants, a car detailing shop, and a small car dealership. Those places are where Evea believed Adam spent most of his time.

Adam stood in their four-car garage listening for Evea's footsteps. He could hear nothing but the warm spring air blowing through the mature trees that lined their property. When he felt the area was quiet enough, he began unloading the cash and walked to the east wall of the garage about fifty feet from the door that led to the lower level family room. Once he reached the correct spot, he moved his workbench and lifted up the cement tile where his bulletproof state-of-the-art custom safe was located. The 10x18 safe was more like a storm cellar beneath the house, with built-in compartments for guns, money, cards, and whatever else Adam could get his hands on. As his adrenaline pumped, Adam hurried, racing against time before Evea came looking for him. Adam placed the last stack in its place and was moving the workbench back, when Evea appeared in the doorway of the garage.

"What are you doing?"

Adam turned around, startled and breathing heavily from moving the husky workstation back in its place. "Woe, Sunshine, you can't creep up on a nigga like that! I was looking for some bolts. I need to fix one of my tires, and the damn thing rolled behind the workstation."

Evea just looked at him and laughed. "You're crazy. The house is smelling like a forest fire and you worried 'bout a bolt."

"Yeah, sexy, ya man tried to cook you up something but almost burned the crib down. Let's go out to eat. Your choice!"

Evea replied, "No, it's not my choice. Your non-cooking ass made that choice for me."

They both giggled as Adam pulled her close and laid a soft kiss on her full lips. Evea melted like a pool of sweet milk chocolate.

*****

Adam pulled up to Cedarbrook International Mall in upstate Pennsylvania about three hours from Philly, where the upper middle class and moderately rich dwelled. People were everywhere sporting the latest spring attire and enjoying the nice weather. Mothers and fathers walked the open mall with their overprivileged toddlers wearing designer names they could not even pronounce.

Evea stepped out of the freshly detailed purple and cream

BMW two-seater convertible glowing. She was well within the season. She wore a simple ocean blue and white linen sundress with a pair of Micheal Kors jeweled sandals. Adam was proud to call her his Sunshine. They walked hand in hand talking as they approached the Rain Forrest Cafe, one of Evea's favorite places to eat. The two ordered the Saturday champagne brunch, and then they got lost in the music and chatter of the Rain Forrest.

Kayla and Jason walked the streets of the prestigious outdoor mall, while talking about the future and the next party going on at their school. They exited the Polo store and decided to head toward Eatery Row where all of the hottest signature restaurants were housed.

"Jason, why you choose me out of all these other uppity chicks on ya back?"

Jason was half black and Latino with dark skin and a sly accent. All of the girls in Kayla's school wanted to be on his arm.

Jason looked in Kay's eyes and replied, "I like rare, one-of-a-kind things in my collection, and you're one of a kind."

Kayla snatched her hand away, and in her Evea attitude, she said, "Oh, so I'm part of a collection? Nigga, please."

As Kayla began to storm off with Jason in tow, she spotted Evea, and Evea saw her, too.

"Hey, Kay-kay," Evea yelled, "where you running to?"

Kayla approached her mother. Looking like Evea's reflection, she had grown to be so beautiful. She was now a teenager and built like a brick house. She had long, thick hair

48

pulled off of her face with an oversized headband. Kayla stood about 5'5" and was about a size 12, plump in all the right places. She was loved by boys and hated by females. Kayla had Evea's bright eyes and Té's complexion. She also had his fire and street smarts. ,

"Hi, Mom, what you doing here?" Kayla asked once she reached her.

"I'm here with Adam. He's getting the car. Who is your stalker?"

"That's Jason, who's about to be my ex-boyfriend."

Jason made it to where Kayla was standing. Out of breath, he asked, "Why you leave me?"

Evea looked him up and down, then said,

"The word is hello."

Still not acknowledging Evea, Jason asked Kayla, "Is this your sister? 'Cause y'all look just alike!"

In an agitated voice, Kayla replied, "No, this is my mother."

Jason looked like he had swallowed a bowling ball. "Oh, I'm sorry, Mrs. Jordan."

Just then, Adam pulled up. Evea said her goodbyes and told Kayla to call about coming over for dinner. Adam waved at Kayla, and she returned the favor as the purple luxury car disappeared into the distance.

Kayla then turned to finish her rage, when Jason said, "You're pretty just like your mom! Your dad is quiet, though."

She felt a pull in her stomach just by the mention of the word dad. She stared into space as she remembered her father and the emptiness she felt since his passing. She hated not knowing anything about his death.

"That's not my dad. Not even close..."

Chapter 5

"Mmmm, mmmm," Peaches moaned, while arching her back up off of the bed. She felt kisses that made their way from her head down to her belly button. The smell of flowers filled the air from a cracked window that anchored the room. Sheer navy blue curtains brushed over her fully naked body. Peaches cracked one eye to be sure she was not dreaming. The view made her heart skip a beat for more than one reason. Looking back up at her was a sexy, hard body of the male species. She blushed as he got closer to her pearl. Back and forth her waist moved, and his face followed in a perfect rhythm. His oversized hands palmed her ass as he pulled her closer to his mouth. He acted as if he wanted to consume her very core. Each slurp and gentle lick sent Peaches' mind spinning and her body craving more contact.

"I can't take it! Give it to me now!" she yelled, shaking as her love juices streamed down his chin. With her screams of passion, she got acquainted with the neighbors.

G gave her exactly what she begged for--more of him. With every muscle in his arms exposed, he picked Peaches up and wrapped her legs around his waist. She was so excited that she rode his love muscle as he walked across the floor. G reached the edge of the doorframe that led to the master bathroom and wedged his body on an angle. Peaches moved up and down, back and forth all at once. G grabbed her hips to guide his lover to the places he wanted to feel. Her moans along with his grunts and squeals sounded like a perfect love ballad. They used each other's bodies like a ride at the amusement park. Totally entertained, they exited the ride together, moaning and giving each other praise as their bodies lay on the six-inch plush carpet shaking from their voyage. Their silence spoke volumes.

Peaches looked up at the high ceilings of the beautifully decorated condo and said to herself, *What a way to get awakened in the morning. I can get used to this real quick.*

Before long, Peaches fell fast asleep.

While awaiting her to wake from her slumber, G hopped in the shower and then handled some business afterward. He'd been having trouble sleeping since he returned home to society from that shithole he called home for years. So, he could not close his eyes for too long.

G sat there staring at Peaches while she slept peacefully. He could not believe her girlish beauty. G was no slouch when it came to looks, smarts, and charm, but he paled in comparison to the charm that Peaches possessed. G had other girls come and go, but never was he willing to wait for them to finish sleeping. G and Peaches had talked for hours the night before when he rescued her from her crazy ex-boyfriend and the embarrassment at the party. He felt a thing for Peaches ever since their encounter at the mall. When you mix drinks and soul-to-soul confessions, you get hot sex on a platter. G felt close to Peaches after saving her from her past.

G was hardcore and one of Té's closest friends before he got locked up. He was one of the original components of their crew. They were more like brothers, having grown up on the same block and attended the same schools all the way through high school. G got knocked some years back because he got involved with the wrong female, and it almost cost Té his life and freedom. So, instead, G walked off the time for him.

Having a weakness for a damsel in distress, G was drawn to Peaches, but he feared all females were conniving, money-hungry whores. With a sudden dose of reality, he thought, *Damn, I just met this chick. She seems sweet, but she could be one of those set-up bitches.* G was snatched back to the present when Peaches' phone began to ring. That's when G yelled for her to wake up and threw the phone at her.

"Yo, you got to get up. I got places to be, and ya phone loud as shit!"

Peaches sat up and tried to get her eyes to focus so she

could make out the number. She wondered where her sweet love warrior went and where Mr. Dickhead came from.

"Hello," Peaches said, trying to clear her throat.

"Bitch, where you at? I been calling your house and texting your ass since last night's crazy episodes!"

"Tiff, slow down. I'm not at home."

"I know that, smart ass. I hope you're not out fucking your next stalker. Keep that pussy to ya'self!"

"Tiff, you're crazy. I'm getting in the shower and will meet you at my house in a few. Bye."

G stood over Peaches. "Naw, shawty, you gonna have to shower at home. I have to go."

Confused with G's new attitude, she gathered her clothes and got dressed while he stood there clocking her moves.

On her drive up the expressway, Peaches was sobbing so hard that the people in other cars could hear her. Being naive, Peaches thought G was into her and that they were going to start dating. They had talked for hours and shared a lot of things about their past and dreams for the future. Peaches felt like a fool. She could barely hold on to the steering wheel for being weak from crying.

Peaches had told G all about Jhamal and their twisted relationship. She explained that he was aggressive in bed and wanted her to hurt him with things. She also explained that he was very possessive and vowed to kill her if she ever left him. Peaches even shared with him about Jhamal wanting her to cut him with a blade when he got close to climaxing one time while they were having sex. When Peaches refused, he smacked her across the room. Peaches felt so low. At this point, she regretted having shared those things with G, who was pushing her away. She hadn't even shared such intimate details of her life with her friends.

What's wrong with me? she thought. *I'm so messed up. I go from stalker boy to having a one-night stand. I got to get it together. He sure got a nice shot, though.*

*****

Tiff prepared herself for a girls' talk with Peaches. She could not face the fact that the spring reminded her of Lex more than she admitted, no matter how busy she tried to keep herself. Tiff jumped out of the shower and put together her cute "I'm not dressed" clothes. She sported a jeweled baby doll tee, a pair of skinny leg Seven jeans, and her mini Gucci wristlet.

After hopping in her ride, Tiff made her way across town. Still not feeling the way Noah was gambling and not taking care of his business, she placed a call to shake things up.

"Hello, nigga. Where you at? What, you forgot where you live?"

"Shawty, what you mean? I'm gud, just handling some business. I'm gonna get wit' you later."

"Yeah, okay, nigga. Don't play with me. I took this pussy off the market for your ass. It only takes a few seconds to get back in the game, and then your pussy turns into my 'do what I want' pussy!"

"Shawty, you always gotta see whose stick is bigger. I catch you when I get home. Oh, and have my pussy hot and ready. One."

Noah hung up, and Tiff was left staring at her phone. Her love pocket was throbbing and wet just from the thought of Noah and his power hitting it from the back.

After walking up to Peaches' door, Tiff rang the bell. The door was opened and the session began.

Chapter 6

The day was moving so fast. It was sunny out, but the sky would soon swallow up the sun and let the moonlight shine. The crew was preparing for the meeting of the dons. They were going all out. Every one of them were getting new clothes and putting on their best underwear. They had a meeting to attend, but not just any meeting. They thought it was time to bring G up to speed and let him take his rightful place in the organization during their annual leader meeting. The crew was no mob, just a bunch of West Philly's finest that had a dream of making it out of the hood and living self-sufficient. They fell into the coke game when G and Té started their business back in high school. One by one, they put their homies on, and now they all were eating in the game that they felt raised them. Most of them had legit businesses, too, except Corn and Noah, who just didn't care about looking the part.

One at a time, the crew showed up at their West Philly hangout in all types of exotic cars and dressed to kill. The spot they were going to was so special that they only did it once a year due to the grip it cost. They reserved the location just for the leader meeting. Corn was leading the line of cars as they mounted up and headed for Reading, Pennsylvania. G rode with Corn as they sang along and bumped to classic Biggie. The sky had turned dark, and the stars were bright as ever. G felt good to be back in the company of true friends.

Corn pulled up in the driveway of what looked like a well-kept farm with so much land about ten houses could be built around it.

G looked at Corn and asked, "What the hell is this? We gonna milk some damn cows now? Not in my good shit. When you said the barn, I thought you was playing."

Corn just looked at him and laughed. As Corn turned right past the beautiful red barn, G could not believe his eyes. Fifty foot trees protected the gated empire.

G's mouth was wide open. "Damn! Dis ain't no barn!"

"Yes, it is," Corn replied. "BARN stands for Beyond Any Reality Now!"

G just laughed as they gave each other dap.

Corn pulled up to the oversized gold gates and pressed a code in the number pad. A lady's voice sounded through an intercom. "What dairy would you like, milk or eggs?"

Corn replied, "Four eggs, please."

The huge gates swung open, letting in all four cars ushered by Corn's burgundy Benz coupe. The driveway was paved with beautiful outdoor tiles that looked like black and gray granite. They pulled into the reserved parking area and were greeted by a six-foot amazon beauty wearing nothing but glitter and pumps.

"Right this way, gentlemen" The lady spoke in a soft, sensual voice with an accent.

The doors of the BARN were opened, and the boys walked through getting much love from the ladies. The hostess led the men past the indoor waterfall and bar stocked with all top-shelf liquor back to their private area. Once they all reached the ten-foot double mahogany doors, Natalia, their hostess, opened them, and the men entered a different world.

The room was huge with a private bar, dance floor, and an enormous black lacquer oval table. Each pure butter-soft leather chair had their names on them. In front of each chair was a box of imported cigars, a bottle of Hennessy, a touchscreen phone, and two hundred thousand in chips for gambling. Their bartender wore a customized tuxedo vest, and the clean-up girls wore the same vests with matching black diamond g-strings. Once the men

took their places, the meeting began.

Noah stood up with his glass full and raised high."Well, fellas, let the meeting begin.

First thing, we want to welcome our man home once again. You was missed by the whole squad!" Everyone broke out in cheers, and after they quieted down, Noah continued. "We have a lot of business to take care of. First things first, the numbers are looking wonderful. If we keep running our areas like this, we will all be getting a five-hundred thousand-dollar raise by next year. Love, how is your project going?"

They all sat and listened as Love responded.

"My project is straight. Them white folks spend more money on that pure white girl than groceries. My chic has the inside connect. She met some guy named Ram that promises to be able to get her in all the right places to drop some weight. See, he has a supplier, but he tasted our shit and is ready to do some side business. We have a meeting with him in a few days, or should I say he thinks he has a meeting with just her."

Noah took it all in and replied, "Damn, dude, that's good shit, and you just got up there. I knew them whities would love it!"

Jay-Roc sat quietly and listened to the celebration of all the money making. Inside, he was hurt and enraged that the killer of the man who started their fortune was still at large.

"I'm happy about all the doe, but where's the love? My man Té got killed years ago, and the nigga that did it is still breathing. We need to get focused back on that nigga and his crew. He's not untouchable!"

G stood up and gave Jay some dap. "Dats my nigga, and I feel the same way. I'm home now and ready for war. My man's death cannot be in vain. I won't have it!" G slammed his fist down on the table.

Noah lightened the mood before going further. "Let's calm this action figure down before he breaks some shit in here. Raise your glasses. Salute to our fallen soldier, Té."

They all yelled, "Salute!" and then threw back a shot of Hennessy.

As the meeting continued, G silently vowed to himself not to let his brother down. Just when G thought the night was over, the highlight had just begun. All of the lights went dim, leaving only four bright spotlights shining in the center of the room.

Natalia ushered ten girls of different shades and nationalities into the room, while the fellas lined up and G just sat there.

"Since you just got home, you're first in line," Corn yelled.

G stood up and took his place at the female smorgasbord.

*****

G did exactly what he vowed to do; he got prepared for war. Everyday he thought about what he would do to the scumbag that killed his closest homie. Business went on as usual, and G was back in the swing of things. He felt good about being able to make his money, which allowed him to take care of his mother and other family. He was definitely back on top, but he would feel much better when he evened the score with Adam.

G had some of his own ideas working. He had a connect

that was looking for Adam and trying to locate Evea and Kayla. G was serious about making sure they were all right. He had missed most of Kayla's childhood and felt she was in need of a daddy in her life.

He had a lead on the type of business that Adam ran. Now, all he had to do was find a way inside the circle. G was cocked and ready to blow. He walked daily with a chrome Desert Eagle and a black-on-black .45 caliber. He was not a second-guessing kind of guy. So, whenever G pulled, he would let off until the clip was empty!

Chapter 7

Evea was awakened by her lover's touch. She opened her eyes, and the clock read 7:00 a.m. Evea loved her some Adam, but this morning, she was struggling to get up after a long night of more than enough. He was burning with desire to be inside of Evea one more time. Adam's hands were all over her. She was not even fully awake, and her body was feeling emotions that she did not understand. *Damn, his touch knows what my body wants. He got me shaking already.* Just as the thought entered Evea's mind, she was brought to a full orgasm.

"Baby, here I come!"

Adam continued to explore Evea's body, sucking her perky

nipples while applying the right amount of pressure to her clitoris with his index finger.

Enjoying himself, Adam said, "Damn, E, you got another one in you. I can feel it."

He was referring to the tension in Evea's pearl, which had grown at least two inches from his hand stroke. Adam liked to watch Evea enjoy herself; he got off more than her. Just as Evea was at her peak again, Adam rolled her shaking body over and placed her perfectly on top of him. Evea, being an award-winning rider, started bucking and gyrating on top of Adam like she was crazy. He lost control, and it was Evea's show. He moaned as his arms fell to his sides.

"You gonna let that dick nut! Come on, give me what I want, daddy!" Evea did a full split while still bouncing on all nine inches. Adam's head started to tingle, and his shaft got harder as Evea contracted her tight walls all around it.

"Baaaaaaabyyyyyy!" Adam sang. "Here I go!"

Evea could not respond. She on her way to having a third orgasm, and Adam knew it. He reached up, grabbed her by the throat, and applied just enough pressure to take her over the top. They both exploded together. Evea fell on top of Adam's chest smiling and exhausted before her day began.

*****

Evea managed to get out of the door and into her pink pearl Lexus coupe. She hated traffic, and most of all, she hated to be late. Evea was on her way to her new gig in upstate

Pennsylvania. Less than ten minutes away, she experienced a major backup. A car was stuck on the only two-way road that led to her job.

"Shit! This has to be a nightmare!" Evea yelled. "I'm tired and hate starting my day late. This shit is crazy."

Evea looked to her left at the perky Caucasian woman who was staring at her and smiling. Evea did not know her; but the car looked familiar. One thing Evea knew was cars and clothes, especially when they were worth remembering. This was no ordinary ride. Everything was custom down to the initials in the tire rims. It was the latest iridescent white Z46 sports car with all the upgrades. Evea had seen the car parked down the road from her in a driveway, which explained why the lady was pointed in the opposite direction towards Evea's home. The traffic began to move, and Evea was elated. She gave a smile back and continued down the road.

She arrived at Muncie Correctional Facility with ten minutes to spare. She pulled in the parking lot and parked in her reserved parking spot. Evea had moved up in ranks and was running her department. She had some years in the system, and once she was convinced by Adam to move upstate, she began working as a lead therapist in the maximum security all-women prison.

Evea hurried from the car, putting her four-hundred-dollar pumps to work. She had a nine o'clock session with an inmate that was on red alert due to the sentence she had just received. When Evea made it to her office, Andrena was already sitting on the chrome bench anchored in the wall. A female CO accompanied her, and she looked like she had been dragged through the mud.

"Good morning, CO Benson. Good morning, Andrena. I will be with you shortly."

Evea entered her sterile cream-colored office and sat her files on top of the file cabinet. Andrena entered the office, and Evea asked her to sit in the chair that sat directly in front of her desk. Evea began by asking how her week had been, and then she went into what Andrena was feeling about her sentence and why. As Andrena sat there pouring her heart out about all the people she would miss while incarcerated, Evea began to think that she was in prison herself. She had no contact with friends and barely dealt with anyone new since her and Adam left without a word. After Evea discussed coping strategies with Andrena, the CO escorted three more inmates in for individual sessions.

The day moved quickly, and it was time for Evea to take a break. So, she wrapped up her last session and headed out for lunch. She walked the long, white hallways and had to make it through several checkpoints. Evea passed a multipurpose room that was filled to capacity. She poked her head in and asked CO Rogers what was going on. CO Rogers explained that the CO training and demonstration was for a new SWAT technique that was just approved, and they had chosen Muncie as one of the pilot locations. It was officers from all over in attendance. Evea took the information and moved on. Listening to her stomach growl, the rest of the information could wait.

Evea's chocolate brown pumps clicked as she walked down the last corridor trying not to look as hungry as she was. She passed the guards at master control as a gust of her smooth fragrance entered their noses. Once she stepped outside, she wished her reserved parking spot was closer. The sun danced off her powder pink and chocolate brown tailored two-piece suit. As she made her way to the car, she saw several more officers lingering in the parking lot. This was a rare occurrence at Muncie Correctional Facility due to the distance from all civilization.

Evea hit the expressway and made it just before the lunch special ended. She pulled up to the seemingly deserted cafe and parked close to the entrance. Once she exited her vehicle, the soft leather reclaimed its original form. When her phone rang, she tried to answer it, look at her watch, and walk all at once. The door swung open, and she seized the opportunity to enter hands free.

"Hello," she yelled into the receiver, but no one answered. So, she placed her cell back in her most coveted possession-- her leather white-on-white Louis Vuitton signature clutch.

The place was at its capacity. Lively waiters dressed in purple and black scurried past tables, taking and delivering orders. The fifty-foot handcrafted cedar wood bar in the center of the room was littered with important people dressed in expensive tailored suits. Evea excused herself all the way to the back corner where she heard whispers of her name coming from. As she got closer to the whispers, her eyes lit up at the sight of her caramel pleasure.

"Hey, sexy," Evea said as she leaned in and placed a soft kiss on Adam's puckered lips.

"Sunshine, you look and smell good enough to eat."

"Didn't you eat enough of this imported chocolate this morning? Too much candy is bad for you!"

They both shared a laugh and playful touch.

Adam's slick ways and smooth talk still brought gushing rivers between Evea's thighs after all those years. Evea took her seat, and they did what they had done at least three times a week since moving into their new life.

Adam sat and watched Evea eat, taking a bite or two in between talking. He could tell something was wrong and wanted to find out what Evea was thinking. Adam had been so involved with Evea since Té's death because he was protecting his investment. He figured if she got close to others at her job or in their neighborhood, he ran the risk of losing her. He feared if she ever found out about what really happened the night of Té's death, he would be without his love for sure.

Evea chatted about her job and the idea that she missed Tiff so much and how she wanted to know if she was still alive. As Evea spoke, Adam thought back to the night when he escaped just before any cops arrived at the murder scene. Just the mention of Tiff's name took him back to the day of Té's funeral when Tiff was the target and shots rained down at the burial like a severe thunderstorm.

"Adam, you there? Adam!"

Evea broke Adam's daydream.

"Sunshine, I want to tell you something. I'm ready to take

that next step with you."

Desperate to have an assurance of keeping Evea, he began to push the idea of marriage as he had done in the past.

"Are you asking what I think you're asking?" Evea replied. "'Cause I just might be ready to move on..."

Before she could finish her sentence, Adam stopped her and said, "Hold that thought. We can finish this tonight."

Lunch was over, and they both left on cloud nine. While speeding back to work after having an hour and a half lunch, she repeated Adam's first and last name with Mrs. in the front until she made it to her reserved parking spot.

Chapter 8

The day was warm, and the air felt like Egyptian cotton blowing against Julie's face. She made her way to her silver two-seater Jag, heading to her fake home after picking up a few items from the nearby mall. Shopping and chocolate, among a few other things, were her weakness. She did not just like chocolate for nutrition; she craved the eye-candy chocolate. Her newfound boy toy and business associate was all man. Julie panted at the thought of Love pounding her petite white ass one more time.

Julie was half-Italian and half-Greek. She grew up in an upper middle class home and attended the best schools money could buy. She possessed an MBA from Princeton University and was a legit businesswoman. She met Love at a mutual bank while he was there making a sizable deposit. Julie, being trained by her alcoholic, money-grubbing mother, could smell money with a sinus infection.

When she spotted Love standing there in his Gucci pants suit and Italian leather loafers, she was speechless. Never had she seen such beautiful, well-dressed eye candy that wasn't gay. She just had to make a move! She always had a thing for dark meat, but was afraid to bring one home. However, Julie figured the money would blind her mother to color when she took him home. Little did Julie know, Love wasn't the type to take home to mother.

After they both made their drops, Julie approached him as he exited the building. Her medium-length chestnut brown bob framed her exotic pretty face perfectly. She slid toward him in her most sexy walk in a pair of 3-inch Manolo's. Love, not being a fan of white girls, never gave her a second glance, but Julie was savvy at getting noticed. By the time Julie finished rubbing up on him and flirting, he accepted her number. Love knew this girl was different, but he never imagined how different.

Julie pulled up to the well-manicured lawn and proceeded to take her bags inside the house. As she approached the double stained glass doors, Love met her on the steps.

"Damn, girl, you was supposed to be here an hour ago! Where the hell you been?" Love was more agitated than upset. When he looked at the Bloomingdale's bag, it provided his answer. "You just had to stop at the mall."

Julie looked up at him with those big bedroom eyes. On fire inside, she wanted Love to take that frustration out on her ass. "Love, we have at least another hour…"

Love cut her off. "We don't have shit. I arrive an hour early. I'm not going into this shit sideways. Now bring ya ass!"

Julie resented that Love talked to her like she knew nothing about the game. She was well versed in the dope game; she had her supply in the family. Her two male cousins that she grew up with had been using pretty Julie to bait customers for years before she ever met Love.

"Okay, okay, I got you. Are we taking my car?"

Love replied, "No, follow me."

They locked up and hopped in Love's olive green Acura truck. As soon as they touched the back road they had to travel to get to the spot, the rain began to fall. Julie sat in the passenger seat admiring her man. She was in need of some sexual healing. Love was vibing and listening to classic Naz, which always put him in his zone when he was on a mission. Fifteen minutes later, they pulled up to the spot and parked next to some trees blending in with their surroundings. Love was relieved they were early.

Julie looked at Love and began arching her back while rubbing her inner thigh. Love just sat and watched the show. Julie's sex drive and adventurous nature is what kept Love coming back for more.

"Shawty, are you serious?" Love tried to appear tough, but his manhood didn't lie. He was definitely excited.

"I am more than serious, Lo," she replied, calling him by her pet name for him.

Before Love could refuse, Julie was on her knees and leaning over her seat. She unbuttoned Love's denim with no hands. She loved to ingest him.

"Ohhhhh, I can't wait to taste you!"

Love could not resist. Julie was a pro, and she did not waste any of his juices. She gently started at his nut sack, licking in small, controlled circles. Her right hand massaged his muscle with each lick. By this time, Love was laying flat and defenseless against her soft mouth. Julie moved up to the head and sucked like she was eating a cherry Blow Pop. Her right hand disappeared, and she was giving head hands-free like a Bluetooth device. Her right hand flicked and played with her wetness. The more he moaned, the closer she came to an orgasm.

"Damn, girl, your mouth should be bronzed and shit," Love said in a shaky voice.

Julie continued to slurp and gurgle as his babies found a new home.

Beep! Beep! Beep! Her cell phone scared them both as they came up out of their orgasm coma. Julie struggled to regain her focus.

"Jewelz speaking."

"What it do, shawty?" a country voice said on the other end.

"You tell me. Are we still on for dinner?" Julie spoke in code.

The voice replied, "Yeah, we gonna do the early bird special. It starts in like ten minutes. Just hold my seat, ya heard me?"

Julie paused and then responded, "Got it." After disconnecting the call, she wiped her mouth and began to fix her clothes.

Love was still getting himself together when Julie told him that Ram had just called and would be there to pick up the product in ten minutes. Love could not say it, but he was glad they made it there early. Still, he wondered what Ram was up to that he had to come early. Love climbed in the backseat and awaited his arrival. Armed with a nine millimeter in one hand and a back-up glock in the small of his back, Love was ready for war, if need be.

Shortly after the phone call, like clockwork, a shinny black custom F-150 with 23-inch rims and royal blue leather interior pulled up bumping Gucci Man. Ram jumped down from the cab and approached Julie, who was standing about fifteen feet from her car. Ramir was from the dirty south, and his talk and attitude showed it. He was about 5'8", light brown with bright eyes and full lips.

"What it do, shawty?" he asked after approaching her. "Let's get this thing popping. You got my work?"

Julie looked at his mouth as if she was trying to understand him with each word. Trying to act nonchalant, Julie replied, "What's up, Ram? Of course, I got it, and why you in a hurry and shit?"

Ramir studied her for shady behavior. "Why you questioning me, shawty? Just handle this. I will have an answer for you in a day or so."

When the lyrics "I'm dressed in all black" rang from Ramir's iPhone, he reached in his pocket to answer it. "What it do, playa?" Julie stood there waiting for him to hang up, while not wanting to seem like she was eavesdropping in on his conversation. Ramir continued. "Yeah, playa, I got da message. 'Bout ta get wit' ya in a few. Easy."

After Ramir hung up, he turned his attention back to Julie. "Like I was saying, shawty, I got you in about a day. If this shit is as good as you say, my next order will have to be delivered on Noah's ark!"

They exchanged packages, and then Ramir and Julie parted ways.

After Julie made it back to the car, Love came out of hiding Love's mission was complete. He always stayed steps ahead of the competition. He had a name and face of their new business connect. What he could not figure out was how a country-ass nigga like Ramir had connects with the upper class white folk.

The drive home was silent as they both attempted to shake off the session that took place a few minutes prior. About five cars up, Love spotted a truck that looked exactly like Ramir's. Love sped up to catch the license plate. As he read the first three, LCA confirmed his suspicions. He did not need to read any more. Julie was now lying back with her eyes closed, listening to her iPod. Love called her name, but she was in her zone, bobbing her head and swaying side to side.

Love nudged her. "J, take that shit off!"

"What's wrong?"

"Yo, didn't you say your cousins knew this nigga from Philly?"

"Yeah, why?"

"Then why I see his ass headed the opposite direction toward where we're headed?"

"Where?"

Love directed her attention to the black truck now four cars ahead.

"Some shit ain't right. I'm gonna drop you off as close as I can get you to home and follow this nigga. I smell some garbage!"

Love kept his distance and grew more anxious as they drove closer to home. Ramir made a turn one block away from their house at a strip mall with a gas station and little convenience store. Love told Julie to get out and make it home. Ramir's truck stopped, and he got out. Julie was trapped. She did not want to risk getting out and being discovered. Love parked on the far corner of the gas station. He was trying to see who or what Ramir was doing in that area.

Ramir walked inside and went to the cashier. Then he came out of the store and continued back to the pump where his truck was parked, while Love sat and watched. After five minutes of filling up, his phone rang and he hopped in his truck. Love was prepared to follow him, when he realized he was not exiting the gas station. Ramir pulled into a parking spot and went inside of the coffee shop adjacent to the convenience store.

Love's adrenaline was pumping. He loved to know things that he was not supposed to know. *Yes, this nigga is sweet. I'm gonna find out his connect in the burbs, too! This shit is too easy.* Love had all types of thoughts running through his head. He was excited to think that Ramir's white connect's identity would be revealed in just a few minutes.

Ramir was inside the coffee shop for a while, but no new cars pulled up. Love told Julie to stay in the car. Then he got out of his truck to position himself away from his vehicle, while getting a closer look. As Love stepped out of the truck, he saw the doors of the coffee shop swing open and a lady exit the building. Inside, Ramir sat with a tall black guy who had black, curly hair. Love tried to see his face, but he couldn't.

Just as Love turned to walk the other way, Ramir stood up to leave. He was headed for the door closest to Love. The mystery man stood up right behind him and began to exit out the other side of the building. Love walked fast to pass Ramir and view the mystery man. As both doors opened, Love caught a silhouette of the tall man. Without a thought, his hand reached in his waist as his eyes became larger than bus headlights.

POP! POP! POP! POP! Love's nine rang like a four-alarm fire. Adam dove for the ground, and the bag with the coffee shop logo on it went flying in the air, causing money to fly everywhere. Ramir's back was turned, but he spun around pointing and dumping with his chrome and black .40 glock.

Bang! Bang! Bang! The few people in the parking lot dove for cover, and Adam crawled on the ground for safety. He was trying to make it to his special semi-automatic sawed-off shotgun in the compartment under his dashboard. Ramir was shooting at Love as he ran to get his man to safety. Julie pulled the truck up, almost running Ramir over while shooting her lady .380 out the driver's window. Love ran and jumped in the truck, and they sped off still firing shots. The two drove straight past their home headed for the city. This news of the dead being resurrected could not wait.

Adam and Ramir got out of dodge as fast as they could. Adam was bleeding, and Ramir was pretty scraped up from playing with the cement. Ramir was confused; all he could think was why the hell was Jewelz shooting at him, and what did Adam have to do with it. Ramir had plenty of questions, but he had to get Adam to medical help quick. Adam was going in and out of consciousness from losing blood. He managed to show Ramir where he lived. Against his judgement, Adam led him to his crib and gave Ramir the number to his doctor on payroll. Ramir followed through like a trooper.

Chapter 9

Wrapped in her favorite spring blanket and with her phone's ringer on silent, Peaches was sleeping peacefully. As she rolled over to get her last bit of RIM sleep before starting her day, she was awakened by a banging at the door.

Bang! Bang! Bang!

"Peaches! Peaches! I know your ass is in there!" A loud voice she knew all too well woke her from her slumber on one of her only days off. "I'm gonna break this bitch down if you don't get up! I know you giving my pussy away! Open this door!"

She was afraid her crazy ex-boyfriend Jhamal had gone too far, and she knew he was capable of hurting her. Peaches and Tiff had just had a conversation about getting a restraining order and putting that baby .22 to use if a nigga got stupid. Tiff was always trying to toughen Peaches up and make her gangsta.

Too scared to open the door, Peaches sat on her queen-size pillow top bed frozen. She was petrified of what Jhamal might do to her or himself and her. She called Tiff's cell, but no answer. Peaches began to cry, and the obvious thing for her to do never entered her mind, which was call 911. Part of her was still protective over Jhamal and did not want him to go to jail. She just wanted him to leave her alone. Peaches figured if she stayed quiet then he would go away.

"Bitch, I see you want to make me look stupid! I see your car out here! Open this door now or I'm coming in!"

Peaches thought about G and how safe she felt with him. They had not spoken since their encounter a few weeks prior. G had made efforts to check on her, but Peaches ignored his calls due to the humiliation she felt after their one-night stand. Peaches remembered G's words: *I got you, ma. If you need me, call me.* A brick flying through her bedroom window snapped her back to reality. Peaches grabbed her phone off of the nightstand and dialed G's number.

"Yo, ma, what's up?" said a voice still prisoner to sleep.

"G, I'm so scared! This nigga is at my door throwing bricks and shit. I need your help! I know we not together, but..."

G interrupted her. "Ma, no problem. I don't need all that. Give me ya address, and I'm there!"

Peaches gave him her house address and prayed he made it there in time. More banging and threats came from the other side of the door.

"I'm coming in!" A large crash had her neighbors up

Peaches began yelling, "NOOOOOOOOOO! Stop, Jhamal! Go away before the cops come, please!"

While Peaches attempted to hold off the monster, G was at home getting prepared for war. G could not stand to see a man beat on a woman or take advantage of her. He grew up watching his mother go through that with his step-pop. Ever since then, he vowed to always help in that situation. G kept it simple, dressing in a lightweight polo sweat suit and a pair of black-on-black Nike track shoes. Equipped with two hammers, he hopped in his Chevy Impala, which he called the goon whip. It was the car he used when shit was going down.

G took all of the back streets and was in the Chestnut Hill section of Philly in no time. Jhamal was still in a tirade. He had kicked her door so much that the hinges were giving way. G pulled over, got out of the car, and walked toward the scene. Already equipped with a plan, he got prepared. He put one foot on the bottom step of Peaches' front landing. When Jhamal turned around, G gave him a two-piece at the speed of light. Jhamal went flying into the bushes, one shoe remaining where he once stood. G proceeded to stomp him repeatedly.

"Nigga, next time you think about Peaches, think about this ass whooping I put on ya ass!"

A crowd of onlookers gathered closer to see what was going on. Jhamal was defenseless and had nothing to say. G had a flashback to his mother lying in the kitchen bleeding from the mouth after one of his stepfather's epic ass whoopings. He lost it, and out of his waistband came a .45, which he placed in Jhamal's mouth. The crowd backed up.

Peaches ran from her house yelling, "G, no! No! He's not worth your freedom. Come on! No!"

The fear and sincerity in Peaches' voice brought G out of his trance. While Jhamal lay bleeding on the grass, Peaches led G back to her house to get cleaned up. The crowd dispersed, and Jhamal limped to his car with both eyes shut.

Once inside the house, Peaches did not really know what to say. So, she remained silent and assisted G with getting cleaned up. As soon as G undressed, Peaches creamed her panties. He was headed for the shower, but Peaches had more than trauma on her mind. She was falling for G fast. Peaches was left alone with her thoughts as she listened to the water hitting every inch of G's hard frame. She wished she was the water that graced his body for cleansing. In the midst of her freaky daydream, G appeared in the bathroom door clean and wrapped in a towel. She sat admiring his frame as he dried off with his towel.

"Thanks for coming and helping me out," she finally said, breaking the silence.

G looked up, and at the same moment, their eyes connected. They both didn't want to turn away.

"Peaches, I told you that I got you." G was now standing straight up. "I told you that I won't let no nigga hurt you again. I know we shared a lot of shit the first night we hooked up, and you probably was wondering why I brushed you off after sharing like that. I was kind of fucked up over our connection, that's all. That shit was crazy."

Peaches stood up, too. "So you do admit shit was real? I just want to..."

G kissed her in between syllables. Then he turned Peaches around and undressed her from behind. Once he had her in full glory, he just stared at her beautiful body. Peaches reached down and took his swollen loins in her grasp. G was careful to lick every inch of Peaches' body. He had her feeling so high that Peaches laid him back and returned the favor. Finally, G was ready to be inside of her. He rotated her around with her head facing the headboard and entered her nice and slow. The slower he went, the more she begged him to go harder and deeper. In and out he slid, with each of Peaches' cries getting louder. When Peaches' body began to shake, G placed his index finger between her rectum and love pocket. His last thrust brought her to ecstasy. He slid his finger in her secret place, and she came until her juices ran down his stomach and sack. G and Peaches were definitely more than a one-night stand.

Peaches and G lay in each other's arms as their bodies surrendered to sleep. The lyrics to "I'm So Hood" blared from his pants pocket repeatedly until G became so annoyed with the sound that he finally rolled over and grabbed his cell.

"Yo, what's up, dude?"

A voice indicating the call was strictly business spoke clear and instructed G to meet at the spot for an emergency meeting. G just sat there listening as Noah ran down the latest development about Adam being alive. The rest would wait for the meeting.

"Sweetie, I got to go, but this will not be our last time together. Your problem should be solved for good now. Don't worry. You're safe. I will check you out later. Be easy."

Peaches had no strength to speak back. G gathered his belongings as he mentally prepared for war, while Peaches lay in their juices speechless, making it evident that she was head over heels for G.

Chapter 10

Evea pulled into the parking lot of her job. The lot looked like a club had let out. She tried to make it to her reserved parking space before they sent the dogs after her. She drove past several officers trying to figure out where to go for lunch, while others made their way to eat lunch in their cars. After pulling into her spot, Evea sat there thinking about what Adam had asked her at lunch. She thought about how long it had been since Té's death, and decided she was ready to move on.

Just then, she said aloud, "Evea, are you ready to give up the name Jordan?"

Evea gathered her purse and other items while thinking about the question she just asked herself.

*****

Tiff walked and enjoyed the visions of her and Noah's encounter last night. Tiff had waited for Noah to get in from his long day of business and gambling. He approached the bed, and Tiff was dressed up like a cheerleader, wearing a red and black cheerleading outfit with matching thigh highs and crotchless panties. Noah was pleasantly surprised to see Tiff in one of her freaky moods.

As Tiff spoke in her cheerleader voice, she moved her bottom around while Noah's eyes were glued to her newly trimmed hot spot. The smell of lilac scented the room and the slow jams played in the background. Tiff stayed in character as she spread her legs wide and rubbed her feather pom-poms against her clit.

"Mmmmm, this feels good, coach. Do you want to play with my pom-poms?"

Noah leaned over to her and began stroking Tiff's walls with his middle finger.

Ring! Ring! Ring! Tiff did not realize her phone was ringing until it was too late. She was startled as she pulled the phone out of her purse and attempted to catch the call.

"Hello! Hello!"

Trying to multi-task, Tiff got knocked to the ground by a car door swinging open.

"Damn, bitch, you can't see! Where you buy your commonsense..." Tiff stopped in mid bark when she found herself staring into the face of her best friend in the whole world. After years of wishing and dreaming about this moment, both ladies were speechless. Tears streamed down their faces as they did years ago on the night they both lost the men that they loved. They embraced each other and held on tight. Sobs and hugs were exchanged as if they were the only ones in the parking lot.

Tiff pulled back and looked at Evea to be sure she was real. "You left me all alone, Evea. How could you do that? I missed you so much year after year, thinking you were dead or in another country. And Kayla, where is she? How could you keep her from me all this time? How did you get out here? Why did you just leave me after the funeral?"

Evea was so emotional that Tiff's sobbing and words were heard through muffled ears. As she began to absorb what was taking place, Evea started to speak. "I love you, Tiff, and I never meant to hurt you. You're my sister. I missed you every day that we were apart. I'm so sorry I could not tell you where I was. I did it for your safety, though. I am soooo sorry."

She squeezed Tiff as if she were holding on for her life. In a sense, Tiff was her only sister she had, and she was reunited with her again. Evea continued.

"Tiff, I did not want those people that killed TE`é to come after you because of me. After they tried to kill you at the funeral, I was so scared me and Kayla was next."

Tiff looked Evea in the eyes, thinking Evea was ready for the truth.

However, before Tiff could say anything, Evea continued

speaking. "Adam moved me, Kayla, and mom out of harm's way, and we have been here for years."

Tiff's body stiffened. "Who moved you away? Did you say Adam?"

"Evea, I have to tell you something." Tiff wiped her tears and instantly became protective. "Where are Kayla and your mom?"

"They are safe. Mom lives not far from me, and Kayla is with her."

"Listen clearly. You are sleeping with the enemy. Adam killed TE`é! He is the murderer. I walked up and found a full shootout! Adam was in on it, and Lex was killed in the process!" Tiff shook and cried harder at the mention of Lex's name.

"Oh my God, what do you mean? Lex is dead, too? Tiff, stop saying things like that."

Tiff continued to explain to her long lost friend that the lover she surrendered her body to night after night was the cold-blooded murderer who took her husband of seven years and Kayla's father from her. Evea became sick, and her twenty-five-dollar lunch decorated the pavement. Tiff told her everything down to the type of gun he used to slay TE`é. She explained that Lex was the one who shot Evea trying to get to Adam.

Evea's world had just changed for the worse in a half-hour. She had just been planning her life as Mrs. Artez, and now, she was planning Adam's demise. Evea's body was present, but her mind was gone. After a while, Tiff's words and the chatter around them faded into background noise. She had flashes of her life since she met Adam and played it over and over. Her lust and greed had turned her world *Inside Out*! She was suited up and ready to reclaim her world.

Tiff and Evea planned how Evea would escape and get Adam back all in one shot. Evea sat there going over the ins and outs of their plan. Evea would have to play two roles if their plan was going to work.

Evea returned to work and finished what was left of her day. Tiff gathered herself and returned to training. She planned her strategy of flushing Adam out during target practice.

Once Evea's workday was done, she headed home for some Oscar-worthy acting. Adam had to pay, and maybe with his life!

Chapter 11

The sky went from bright to dim and then pitch black. The sun was gone, and the moon took center stage. Julie had been driving for a few hours and was curious as to where she was taking Love and what she might witness along their journey. Julie was a rider, but definitely not a fool. She and Love came from worlds apart. She was aware of the problems she may face just by her association with him. She drove in silence while listening to the voice in her head. She had just been in a shootout on a quiet suburban street. Julie was no stranger to organized crime, but never had she been so hands on. Love was all the man she wanted, and she was willing to go to the wall for him.

The car coasted along on cruise control as smooth grooves played in the background. Love sat beside Julie with his seat reclined halfway. He had made all his important calls to gather the crew and was eager to arrive at the meeting.

Love stared up at the stars through the sunroof top. He was torn between how much he should let Julie know about him and his crew. Love was a secretive dude that always stayed ahead in the game. He was grateful that Julie was there and she was instrumental in him still being alive. However, he was frustrated because he had to break one of his own rules and include her in the circle. This infuriated Love, and he grew angrier with Adam as the miles melted away.

The dark country-like roads transitioned to well-lit city streets. Love instructed Julie as they came closer to West Philly's hideout spot.

"Okay, sweetie, turn left here," Love said, breaking the silence between the two of them.

Julie obeyed his commands. She drove a little further, and after passing the third traffic light, she pulled into an empty parking spot. Love gave her a look of confusion mixed with agitation.

"What you doing, Julie?"

"I'm stopping!"

"Why? I got to be somewhere in a few minutes."

Julie gave Love a look of control he had never seen with her before.

"Love, I get that you want to keep your business close to chest, but I was just in a fucking shootout with you. I think I deserve an explanation. What the fuck was that about?"

Love sat and looked at Julie for a moment. "J, you don't need to know shit. It's too complicated! Now just drive!"

"Look, dude, I think just almost dying with someone gives me a damn need to know! I set up a coke job and winded up in a fucking shootout with my connect and a guy I know nothing about! A shootout that you started might I add! So, yeah, I deserve some answers."

Love was taken aback by the strength and courage Julie displayed. He positioned his seat completely up and began to speak. "I didn't start shit! That shootout started long before I met you!"

He took a deep breath and began to bring Julie up to speed, while Julie's mouth hung open as the truck became road bound once again. Love had just fallen for the first time.

*****

The night was cool, and the breeze was forgiving. The fellas arrived one at a time. Before long, all the key players were present. They were just awaiting the arrival of Love, who possessed all the information they were looking for. The large well-lit row home sat on the corner of the block. The house was only used to hang out and discuss urgent business. It was located in the center of West Philly and an easy location for everyone to get to in a timely manner. The house inside was painted a burnt orange and tan color. Every room was furnished and equipped with plenty of entertainment. The meeting house was never furnished with any drugs or drug paraphernalia; it stayed squeaky clean. That night, the word was out, and everyone connected to them showed up. The biggest to the smallest soldier was there to hear the big news. The turnout was a true testament to how much Té's crew loved him and respected his gangsta.

After Julie pulled up in the lot beside the house, Love gave her instructions to stay in the car and he would be back to get her as soon as possible. Love exited the vehicle and entered the meeting where the common look on everyone's face was that of concern. As he entered the house, everyone clapped, happy to see one of their own alive after a dangerous situation. Once the claps faded, the meeting began.

Love explained to all the men the details of his run-in with the murderer of their friend. The room was silent as each man absorbed the information. Jay-Roc broke the silence, as he could not take the suspense any longer.

"So you shot that pretty muthafucka! Did you kill his ass?" Jay-Roc's anger consumed him. He had been gunning for Adam since he got Evea shot up, and the thought of him killing the man that was like family to him sent him into a rage.

"I got that nigga good, but I don't think he's dead," Love answered.

G fed off of Jay-Roc's hatred. "So this nigga is still a problem then! I say we set up shop in that area and kill his ass on sight!"

Everyone began to cheer with thunderous voices. Noah

brought order to the group, and Love continued his proposed strategy.

Love was done with his story and proposed solution, when Noah said, "So where is the hero of the story at now? That bitch is a rider!"

Should I let them know I brought this chick with me? Love thought to himself. Reluctantly, he finally responded, "She's in the car waiting for a nigga!"

Love was ready for the crazy looks and judgmental comments, but he received the total opposite.

Noah yelled, "Break out the Hennessy! We need to toast to that bitch 'cause she bad. If she is as good in bed as she is with a gun, she's da one!" He held up an imaginary shot glass and said, "A toast to Snow White!"

They all followed his lead while laughing in unison. Miguel, one of the Spanish crew members, yelled out, "Salute, Blanca!"

From there, Julie was welcomed into the crew and Blanca was born.

Miles away in upstate PA...

"Ahhhhhhhh...shit!" Adam yelled as he gained consciousness. "What the fuck!"

Ramir stood by as he watched Adam bitch about the painful wound on his left shoulder. The petite Asian nurse paid special attention to the wound caused by Love's gun. Adam squirmed as she attempted to sterilize the area to prevent infection. The bullet did not go all the way through his shoulder, but he had a pretty deep flesh wound. Adam had forgotten how painful it was to be shot or grazed by a bullet.

Ramir spoke while holding his laughter back. "You straight, partner? Seem like you fittin' to cry and shit."

Adam gave Ramir a look that could kill. "Nigga, I see you got jokes, but ya country ass don't have no wounds!"

"Yeah, 'cause I been dodging bullets since I was a jit! Practice makes perfect."

Adam could barely understand Ramir's accent and slang half the time. "What the fuck is a jit?" he asked with disgust.

Ramir laughed. "Y'all city niggas are so smart. It's short for jitterbug, nigga, and means youngin'!"

Adam sat blocking out the pain the little Asian woman was causing him. He wanted to beat the shit out of Ramir for his smart comments, but he knew Ramir was a real nigga. Ramir had proved that when he turned around blazing fire back at the nigga shooting at him. So, Adam collected himself and tried to think of Ramir as his new right-hand man.

Ramir faded into the background as the nurse finished working on Adam. He admired how fly Adam was living. He reflected back to their first encounter and how Adam never really let him in. Ramir was a little upset about the fact that the nigga never told him anything about himself and never even kicked it with him, and now everything was different because his ass was shot. Ramir did not trust anyone that was distrusting. He felt a nigga shouldn't give out his security codes, but at least should kick it with a nigga that's supposed to be in the same crew. Now Ramir was sure Adam had plenty to hide, and not just his residence.

The nurse finished up and gave Adam a pain pill to keep him comfortable. Adam gave her compensation in cash and let her out the side door. Turning around too fast, Adam almost fell and had to grab the wall for balance. Ramir was glad the nurse was gone because he intended to find out just who Adam really was.

"So what it do, partner?" Ramir said as an open-ended question.

Adam sat down on his cranberry-colored leather sofa in his study. He looked as if he was looking through Ramir. In reality, he was trying to decide what parts of his life he would share with Ramir.

"Why you staring like you fittin' to faint, nigga?"

Adam broke his stare and cleared his throat.

"Nigga, what you mean 'what it do'?"

"You know what I mean. What the fuck was that all about? Why was that white girl shooting at me and that fella shooting at yo' ass?" Ramir pretended not to know Julie. He was using her as a side hustle, but what he could not understand was what she had to do with Adam.

Adam positioned a couch pillow under his arm to rest it as he leaned forward. "Your guess is as good as mine, Ramir. I don't know either one of them crazy-ass people."

Ramir squinted his eyes as a sign he was not buying the story Adam was feeding him. "So niggas up here just go around shooting at a playa? I don't believe that shit!"

Adam and Ramir both chuckled. The fact was that Adam

really didn't know neither Love nor Julie, but he had enough baggage from his past to guess why someone wanted him dead.

"Look, Ramir, I'm a very private person, and I don't like people in my shit."

"Bro, you put me in yo' shit when I got shot at! What type of busta-ass shit is this?"

Ramir, now visibly angry, stood up and walked toward Adam. He was startled by a slam and then footsteps approaching fast. Ramir placed his left hand in the small of his back to retrieve his Glock. Adam stood up knowing the sound he heard was Evea.

"Shitttt!" Adam said.

Ramir looked at him and asked, "What, man? Who the hell is that?"

Just as he got the last syllable out, a sight for sore eyes graced his presence.

Adam recovered with, "Hey, Sunshine, how was your day?"

Ramir dropped his left hand to his side and stood there thinking to himself, *I hope Sunshine is his sister, 'cause shawty is BAD!* Ramir's eyes scanned Evea's body like a machine at the airport. When Adam caught Ramir's eyes roaming his merchandise, he started to feel vulnerable about someone he worked with knowing about Evea.

He awkwardly said "Ra, this is my wife Evea," Adam awkwardly said.

Evea replied in her seductive voice, "Soon-to-be wife,

sexy."

She thought about Adam shooting her husband in cold blood and had practiced how she would kill him all the way home, but she knew she had to be the best fake bitch alive. So, she dove into character.

"Who's your friend? And what happened to your arm?"

Evea was more interested in the first question. While Adam thought about Evea's question, she did Ramir the favor of returning his stare. Ramir was not as tall as she liked her men, but he was fine in his own right. Adam thought about Evea's question.

"Oh, baby, I told you his name is Ra...well, Ramir. He works for me at one of the detailing shops." Adam wanted Evea to think less of Ramir, who he knew was capable of being his competition. "Ra just drove me home 'cause I hurt myself on one of the machines at the site. He was just leaving."

"Awww, let me see ya boo boo." Evea approached him to get a look at his shoulder, but he pulled his arm back so she would not touch the bandage.

"No, sweetie, it needs to stay covered!"

Evea backed away. She could smell the gunpowder on him when she got closer. This familiar smell took her back to the night of her terrible shooting years prior.

"Okay, baby. I will go start dinner then." She sashayed away from Adam as Ramir's eyes tried to remain tamed. As she approached the doorway of the study, she looked over her right shoulder and seductively said, "Nice to meet you, Ra.

Guess I will see you again." Evea's shadow disappeared, and Adam sent Ramir on his way.

As Evea cooked dinner, she placed a call to Tiff with the news.

"Hello," Tiff yelled into the phone.

"T, you not gonna believe this. I got home and Adam had some new fine nigga in our crib. He never brings anyone home with him. And on top of that, he smells like gunpowder and is all bandaged up."

"Who smells like gunpowder, the fine nigga? Shit, I love a bad boy!"

"Damn, Tiff, things never change. Even in a situation like this, you thinking 'bout dick! No, Adam is bandaged. Now focus."

Tiff took all of the information in.

"E, I told you that nigga ain't shit! He's into some crazy shit. Remember, when this is all over, we gonna get you a pair of how-to-spot-a–nothin'-ass-nigga glasses!"

They both laughed, which was a sound that Evea or Tiff had not heard in many years.

Chapter 12

Kayla awoke to an annoying alarm along with her grandmother yelling for her to hurry up and get ready for school.

"Okay, Grandma! I'm awake, just like the rest of the neighborhood!"

Her grandmother replied, "Don't think 'cause we out of the hood I won't go hood on ya! Now watch ya tone, girl!"

Kayla laughed at how her grandmother would try to sound hip. Most times, it worked. She was one of the coolest grandmothers around, and she was a fairly young grandma-- only fifty-three years old. She was young when she gave birth to Evea and raised her by herself. Kayla had been close to her ever since she was a little girl. She loved spending time with her grandmother but did not like the domestic side of spending time. No, Kayla was more of the business-minded type like her daddy and Evea. She had just a little more grit than her mother.

Kayla followed her grandmother's directions and slid out of the bed. She had been feeling down for the past few days and was looking forward to having dinner with her mother and Adam that evening.

Kayla may have been gritty like Té, but she got her style from her mother. Although she had been thinking about her father a lot more and wondering why his death was such a secret, clothes and dressing up always cheered her up. So, she thought about what to wear to school. She had to be perfect; that was one of her mother's rules since she was a little girl. The day was special to her because she was spending the afternoon with Jason, her boo. Therefore, Kayla was faced with the challenge of looking good all day and being presentable for dinner with her mother.

She sat on her soft queen-size bed as the light played peek-a-boo with her through the custom shabby chic draperies. Her room had the perfect girly touch, but it was not a kiddy room. The hot pink walls were framed with jet-black baseboards. Her bed and other accessories were hot pink with black and white animal print.

Kayla rose from her bed and entered her walk-in closet. Sitting on her lounge chair in the center of her wardrobe room, she sized up her choices. After ten minutes had passed, she made her decision. Kayla adorned her frame with a pair of low-rise black Ferragamo jeans with an ocean-blue baby doll tee splashed with black and silver writing for the logo. She topped her look off with some satin ocean-blue, gray and white high-top Gucci sneakers. Her hair was in her latest razor-cut bob. She was ready for whatever the day would bring.

*****

The morning started off slow. Evea could not sleep. She tossed and turned throughout the night, having dream after dream about the harm she had brought to her family. She rolled over to find that Adam was missing; his side of the bed lay cold. She sprung up, searching the bedroom suite for him.

"Adam, where are you?" she yelled, trying to be sure she was alone before searching through his things.

Even though Tiff had told her everything, she wanted it all to be a lie. She desperately wanted things to be normal and Adam not to be the murderer that he was. When there was no answer from Adam, she decided to look downstairs before she began to search through his drawers and his study. Each step cracked a little louder as she tried not to make noise. Adam was nowhere in plain sight.

Adam had risen early feeling brand new. The pain pills he received worked wonders, and he wanted to place the money and other items that Ramir had given him in a safe place. He knew Evea was not due to get up for another hour.

As Evea approached the door that led to the garage, she prepared herself to act on cue when she saw Adam. She talked herself into burying the hatred that had began brewing twenty-four hours prior. Turning the corner, she saw no sign of Adam. What she did see shocked her. Adam's workbench that was supposed to be custom mounted to the garage wall was slightly moved away, and she could see a light shinning from a crack in the wall.

"What the hell is this?" Evea said out loud.

She approached the light closer and discovered what looked like a secret hideaway of the house. Not paying attention, she tripped over a tool laying in the walkway. Not wanting to be discovered by Adam, she ran back in the house and up the stairs as quickly as possible.

Thinking he heard a noise, with his weapon drawn, Adam hurried out of the room containing the safe. When he saw the coast was clear, he immediately entered the house to see if his nightmare had come true--Evea finding out about the real him. Once he passed his study and then the kitchen, he was relieved Evea was nowhere in the area. He placed his gun in the top drawer of his study and headed up the steps. Reaching their bedroom, he was met by a vision of beauty.

Evea lay in bed with the covers half off of her body, exposing her perfectly round ass in some pink lace booty shorts and her perky breasts pressed against a matching tank. Evea attempted to regulate her breathing to appear as though she was asleep. Adam approached. His soft, full lips kissed her from the ankle of her left leg to the base of her back, sparing not an inch of her silky skin.

"Sunshine," he whispered.

The once seductive and alluring nickname made Evea's skin crawl. She attempted to ignore her lover and act as if she was still held captive by her slumber. Adam was brick hard and not giving up. He rolled Evea on her back and spread her docile legs apart. Adam licked her exposed wetness slowly. She jerked. Her mind and body were at war. She was consumed with hatred and pleasure all at once. Evea hated that Adam held the key to each of her secret places. Evea's eyes opened and locked with her now adversary. Clearing her throat, she got into character.

"Mmmm, baby, that feels nice," she moaned.

Adam continued with Evea's encouragement. "You like that, baby?" he asked, looking for Evea's approval.

"Yes, baby, but we have to be careful. You're hurt, remember? I don't want to mess you up any more than you already are."

Evea was careful to sound truly concerned for him. She was hoping her words of caution would be enough to save her from sleeping with the enemy one more time. Adam's hormones were far ahead of anything Evea could say to him, though.

He looked at her and said, "This pussy is worth every bit of pain. I will take my chances."

Adam massaged and played with Evea's full breasts as he circled her clit with just the tip of his tongue. Evea fought it, but she cried out in pleasure, ushering one orgasm after another. Evea's body lay controlled by every one of Adam's licks and bites. She began to move so fast it was as if she was convulsing. Every nerve in her body was alive to his touch. Adam loved to control her in that manner. He was well versed on all of Evea's spots when it came to making love. The shaking and high-pitched sounds were music to his ears. Adam was certain she was on the verge of a huge climax as Evea bucked her body up fully out of control. Adam traced her sopping wet hole and slid his index finger deep into her forbidden place, while Evea yelled and cried out as if she was freeing her spirit. She seductively begged for Adam to stop, but he had just begun what he considered foreplay. Evea's body lay paralyzed from passion, while Adam stood before her with her sweet juices dripping from his chin.

"I'm not done with you yet, baby. You need to scream my name!"

Evea's battle of hate and love for Adam overtook her. Adam climbed onto the bed, first with his feet planted flat and then in a full squatting position. He pulled Evea close to him with her legs spread wide. Slowly, he entered her as he moved into a frog-like position. He hopped up and down inside of Evea as their pelvises became one. With each bounce, his 9-inch stick hit the roof and base of her vagina. Adam's hops became quicker, and he was about to bring it on home. He exploded, and so did Evea. As she ushered in her final orgasm, tears streamed down her face and stained her heart.

Adam rolled over and got out of the bed so he could get ready to go handle some business for Ramir and meet with a few other associates. Evea remained still as to appear exhausted from that great lovemaking. He felt it would be best to let her sleep until the alarm went off. After all, it was Evea's day to go to work a little later due to her having flex time. While walking toward the beautifully designed master bath, Adam turned around to get one more look at the love of his life.

"How did I get so lucky?" he whispered. Little did he know his luck had run out.

Evea's cries put her in a deep sleep. About an hour later, her alarm went off. She looked at the time and realized she had no time to get ready for work. Evea jumped up out of bed half asleep and sore from her lover's touch.

"Oh shit!" she yelled. "Adam, why didn't you wake me?"

When she ran to the bathroom, she was met with a sticky note on the mirror. It read: *Sunshine, I love more today than I did the first year. I truly cherish you and can't wait to make you Mrs. Artez. I will see you tonight. Love always, Adam.*

"NOOOOOOO!" Evea yelled as she balled the paper up and threw it against the mirror. She was finally coming face to face with what her harmless fling had cost her.

Later that day...

School was out, and Kayla went to the girl's restroom to reapply her lip-gloss. She was hot and ready to spend the afternoon with Jason. Kayla and Jason had become real close.

Ever since the day at the mall when he almost got cut short, Kayla opened up to him about her father and the mystery about his death. She had never done that with anyone before, not even her mother. She held back due to the feelings she knew her mother had for her father.

Refreshed and shining, Kayla exited the restroom and headed toward the school parking lot where her boo would greet her. The green double metal doors swung open, and Kayla's pretty brown eyes sparkled in the sunlight. Jason spotted her as he rested against his ride. Kayla put some seduction in her stride while making her way to her boy toy. Jason stood up to greet her, and when Kayla made it to her sweetheart, she kissed him slow in the mouth. Jason's brain competed with his hormones. Kayla seemed different to him, more relaxed and open with physical boundaries.

After the long kiss, Kayla smiled and said, "Let's ride, boo."

Jason granted her wish and drove a few miles down the road. As he pulled into a pretty sitting park with seasonal flowers in full bloom, Kayla's face had a look of confusion. She was sure they were going to his house while his parents were still at work. Today was the day when she would become a woman. She thought to herself, *I know this nigga don't think he getting no ass in the park. What's good wit' this dude?*

Jason did not speak. He just parked the car and turned the radio down. Kayla became worried.

"Jason, what's this about? I thought we were going to your crib."

Jason wanted Kayla so bad, but the mood would soon not be that of a sexual one.

"Baby, let's get out and walk around and talk."

Kayla just sat there staring at him. "Are you serious? What is this about, Jason?"

Jason replied by saying, "Look, Kayla, I love you so much. I never felt like this about another girl. It just wouldn't be right if I took advantage of the situation."

Kayla stopped him from continuing.

"Jason, I love you, too. I want this, so you're not taking advantage."

Jason reached over Kayla and opened his glove compartment. He pulled out a bunch of black and white papers and handed them to Kayla. As Kayla read the archived newspaper articles, tears streamed down her face. Jason explained that he got curious after they had been talking about her dad so much. He wanted to help her bring closure, but he was not prepared for what he had discovered.

The articles gave every detail about Té's life and death. It talked about how he was a known part of organized crime and how his death was drug related due to the others who died with him. The article mentioned Lex by his street name and government name. He was a known big man but was never caught with anything.

Kayla sat there relieved to know the truth, but hurt by the harsh reality of who her father was. She had just became a woman, but not by physical submission. Kayla gathered herself as Jason held her tight.

"Take me to my mother's house!" she screamed. "How could she do this to me? How?"

Jason backed out of the parking space and headed toward the truth.

Chapter 13

The smell of burnt rubber permeated through the air. The subwoofers thumped as G did almost ninety-five miles an hour up the expressway. He sang along to every song on Biggie's *Ready to Die* album. The more he sang, the faster he drove. A line of at least ten cars littered the expressway scattered throughout as not to seem obvious that they were the Calvary. G chose that particular CD to feel closer to Té. Although Biggie's demise had come a decade plus before that time, he remained one of the best, and he was Té's favorite rapper.

G was on a mission and ready for the outcome. He was ready to put the nigga that took his brother's life prematurely to a final rest. It was no way Adam would make it out alive.

He had to be stopped, and G wanted to be the one to complete the mission. His awareness was on full alert, and he was packing so much heat that if he made a sudden stop, the guns would blaze on their own.

A few cars behind G were Love and Blanca. She was a part of the crew and her name was coined. Love talked to her about what her role would be. He planned to drop her off at home and let her get in full costume. She was just the right color to be seen walking around loosely in the suburban neighborhood. Love went over their plan three more times before he turned the music back to regular volume. He explained to her that she needed to get in good with the chicks in the neighborhood. Love had studied Adam, and he knew females were his downfall. Love told Blanca that Adam had to be living with someone. He also explained how Adam was one of them need-a-bitch niggas that was not about to change. Little did Love know the bitch that Adam needed had been the same bitch for years—the wife of one of his best friends.

The men had been driving for a couple of hours and were about forty-five minutes away from their destination. Everyone had instructions, and Adam would soon see his maker.

Jay-Roc could not contain himself. He was so close to seeing Adam get what he deserved he could taste it. He just kept thinking that all of this had to have a purpose. He thought back to how he watched his friend die in cold blood at the hands of a low-life pretty boy. His jaw muscles tightened up with the thought of that night. He felt so guilty for not running out to bang Adam himself. He remembered getting a few shots off, but none of them were fatal for the nigga. After Té dropped, Jay-Roc remembered lots of sirens, and he and Love were forced to get the hell out of there. Love always told Jay that he did the right thing and that Té would not want them to be behind bars with the nigga still on the run. The day had come, though, and Adam would not be among the living much longer.

Forty-five minutes turned to ten. All of the cars took their places. They had a description of Adam and the car he was driving. Love did not bank on him driving the same car, but he felt it wouldn't hurt to give the description. Love was detailed about Ramir and his ride, as well. He did not want to take any chances at missing the target.

Love entered his street, and the houses looked very different from where he was from. They all were picture perfect. Blanca waved at some of the neighbors she had become friendly with. The street was huge. There were not many houses like the row homes in West Philly, but the street stretched for a couple of miles occupied with well-built single-family homes. Love was making good timing until he was slowed down by a tow truck that could not seem to maneuver a broken down car into the driveway.

"What the fuck, man? Where did this nigga get his license?"

Beeeep! Beeeep! Love blew his horn to try to squeeze past. The tow-truck driver was polite and asked for a little more patience from Love, who opened the car door and exited his vehicle in an attempt to speak to the tow-truck driver with respect. As he reached the driver's door, he backtracked.

"What the fuck!" he yelled.

The driver had prepared himself for the rude comments that Love may throw at him. However, Love was not yelling at him, but rather yelling in the direction of the truck that he was towing. Blanca sat in the front seat of Love's truck with the same look of confusion. Those rims were undeniable. The truck being dropped off on their block at the mystery house was Ramir's. Adam had arranged for it to be picked up and brought to his house so Ramir could claim his ride when he delivered Adam's whip detailed and freshened up.

Love picked up the phone to alert the soldiers. His new information would change everything.

Chapter 14

The tears from Evea's eyes had formed a small puddle beneath her. She had been sitting on the family room floor rocking and crying since mid morning. It was now afternoon and she still could not move. Her cell phone had rung more than twenty times, and the ringing at the door she ignored until it faded away. She felt paralyzed. Every one of her limbs felt too heavy for her body.

She yelled and cried. She asked God for forgiveness and held a small picture that she kept of her and Té tightly to her chest. Repeatedly, she chanted, "I'm so sorry. I can't believe I have been this stupid!" Evea would not be recognized as a professional in the mental health field. She was having a major breakdown. Evea had been staring at her phone for hours, with her mind telling her fingers to dial.

Her body became limp as she rested her head on the soft carpet.

Buzzzz! Buzzzz!

Evea's phone vibrated against her side. She found enough strength to lift her head, and when she saw Tiff's name, she gathered herself.

"Hello," Evea answered in a weak, shaky voice.

"Evea, you don't sound good. Are you okay?" Tiff asked. "Why aren't you at work? We was supposed to be perfecting our plan."

When Evea did not respond, Tiff became worried and her pitch got a little higher

"Evea, what's going on? Talk to me, baby girl. You're scaring me! Did that nigga hurt you?"

Evea's crackling voice calmed Tiff down.

"Tiffany, he took all I had! How could I be so stupid?"

Tiff sat back in her chair. "E, what happened since we spoke yesterday? What happened?"

Evea began to tell Tiff everything, taking breaks to gain her strength. "I saw it all, Tiff. This nigga is into some crazy shit. I woke up earlier and did not see him. When I entered the garage, I noticed a secret crack in the wall where light was shining through. After he left for the day, I went to see what was hidden in the little hideaway. I was not ready for what I saw. It turns out that it's a fucking custom built tomb with millions of dollars in cash, credit cards, credit card machines, guns, and other shit!"

As the last words escaped her lips, she began to sob again.

"Tiff, I found it! I found the gun that killed Té! What sick fucker keeps something like that? I fucking killed my husband. I let an outsider in! I don't deserve to be here. I should have died, not Té!"

Tiff stopped Evea when she began to talk about death. "E, get yourself together. You know what has to be done! Adam has to go!"

Evea continued. "That's not all I found. The gun we both saw sticking out of the car window at Té's funeral...the custom made chrome nine...was there, too. That nigga tried to off you, and I've been lying up with him night after night."

Tiff sat silently on the phone. She had Evea back, but bloodshed was inevitable.

*****

Kayla arrived at her mother's door, passing the tow truck that was leaving the premises.

"I can't believe she lied to me all these years. I'm going to get the truth out of her once and for all." Those were Kayla's last words to Jason before she jumped out of his ride.

She stood there in the doorway of the family room consumed with hatred for her mother and Adam. She could not believe what she had just overheard her mother say into the phone. Adam, her mother's lover for years, was the murderer of her beloved father. Kayla's sheltered world had just spun out of control. *How could my beautiful, intelligent mother be so stupid? Fucking the man that killed her husband?!*

Evea looked up startled by Kayla's presence. Not knowing how much Kayla had heard, she decided to remain silent. Kayla approached her broken down mother and threw the papers at her. They landed in her lap. Evea picked up the papers, and the content gave a reason for Kayla's screams.

"How could you lie to me year after year?! I deserved to know what happened to my father. He was murdered in cold blood, and you never told me the truth. I felt like I was lost not knowing what happened to him. I remember as a little girl I thought he left because of me! How could you?"

Evea sat there crying and reaching out to her hysterical daughter. "I wanted to protect you! Kay, I'm sorry. I love you."

Kayla looked into Evea's already broken eyes with hatred and disgust. "Like you loved my daddy? No, thank you!" Kayla stormed off and left her grieving mother all alone.

Evea was broken, but Kayla's rage snapped her out of her crying frenzy. She refused to let Adam take away her daughter, too. He had to pay, and that was what he was going to do!

Evea's phone rang several more times. It was Adam calling her. She knew he would be home soon, especially since she did not answer. Evea was blessed with a newfound strength. She reentered Adam's hideaway and ushered millions after millions of dollars out of his safe. Evea placed the workbench back in its place, being sure to leave the secret room cracked as she found it earlier.

After making it upstairs, she gave herself a beauty makeover. Evea placed cucumbers over her eyes and soaked in her expensive body fragrance. She was having a party, and the guest of honor would be Adam. She wanted to look good for his last soiree. Evea's plan was set, and she put it in motion. She made her first call and drank a glass of wine to celebrate before making her second and final call.

"To sweet revenge." Evea held up her two-thousand-dollar Cristal and toasted to the air.

*****

Love was so excited after his call. The plan was changed. Everyone was meeting at his spot and waiting until nightfall to strike. One thing he knew, somebody was going down. He could not believe Ramir lived on the same street. Little did he know his main target was right under his nose. Love had an iron clad plan, which consisted of kidnapping Ramir from his house and making him lead them to Adam. He could not wait to even the score. An eye for an eye, and two lives for his homie's life. Revenge was gonna be sweet!

Chapter 15

Tiff stepped out of the shower one leg at a time. While passing the mirror, she admired her ass. She was on a mission, but she could not resist herself. Probably one of the reasons she could masturbate on the spot. Tiff stepped to her bedroom quickly and made it to her bed where her outfit awaited to be placed on her small frame. Tiff swooped up her now long hair into a ponytail. Then she stepped into the all-black Versace catsuit, admiring how soft the silk felt against her naked skin. Tiff placed her black Kenneth Cole knee-high boots on one at a time. She strapped her snub-nose handgun in her boot holster and then placed her lady .9mm in her side holster, concealing it with a smoke gray and black vest. After double-checking her purse for her keys and placing her Avenger jagged-edge martial arts knife on the other side of her holster, Tiff was ready for war. She headed out the door right on time.

On the way out of the city, she called Peaches and gave her the brief version of the story. Peaches was a part of the girl squad, but was not in tune with her gangsta side. Tiff knew what she needed to do, and after talking to Peaches for most of her ride upstate, she told Peaches that she would call her once she got to where she was going. Tiff dialed the number she had to call to clear some things up.

"What up, shawty?" Noah chimed in as he answered his phone.

"Hey, baby, what's good? I just called to say I love you and thank you for putting up wit' a bitch!"

"Tiffany, are you good? What's wrong, baby?" Noah hardly ever called Tiff by her name, let alone her full name. He was concerned. Showing emotions was not one of Tiff's strong suits.

Having been together shortly after Lex got killed, Noah and Tiff helped each other out a lot. They both lost someone they loved that night, and they bonded over that. Over the years, their feelings grew deeper. Tiff was afraid to say anything because whatever she loved always left her somehow. First, Lex and then, Evea. Tiff had hardened her heart to love, but despite her hard exterior, feelings of love and respect had set in for Noah, and she had to acknowledge it.

Tiff took a while before responding. "I'm good, nigga. A bitch can't show you love? I just wanted you to know it's only you, Noah. Real talk."

Noah was choked up. He could not believe what he was hearing from the other end of his phone. "I definitely love you. You my shawty and always will be."

Tiff was ecstatic to hear him say those words. Not wanting the moment to remain so serious, she countered with, "For sure, nigga...you don't love me. You just like my doggy style."

Both Noah and Tiff shared a laugh.

"I'll see a little later, shawty. Stay safe. One."

"Yeah, one love, Noah."

After arriving at her destination, Tiff pulled up to the back and began loading her car up. She left the engine running for a quick getaway.

*****

Evea had finished dinner and was awaiting her plan to unfold. She knew Adam was due home soon, and she was ready to start the party of the year! When she heard a car pull up out front, she rushed to the window. For sure that was Adam's car puling up. She noticed an unfamiliar truck sitting beside the car with the engine running.

"When the hell did that truck get here?" she said out loud.

She continued to stare out of the window, waiting to see Adam and hoping their guest would arrive soon. The car door swung open and out jumped a familiar face, but not Adam. Shortly, the doorbell rang. Evea was thinking quickly on her feet. As she approached the door, she tried to rethink her plan, but she was drawing a blank. She arrived at the oversized front door and opened it.

"Hello, Sunshine," Ramir said.

Evea giggled because he thought that was her real name. It sounded sexy coming from him with his country accent.

"Is Adam here?" Ramir asked. "I was supposed to meet him to pick up my truck."

Evea stared at Ramir like he was something good to eat. Plan B had just dawned on her.

"Oh, that's your truck? I was wondering where it came from. Come in. Adam will be here shortly, and the name is Evea, Ra."

Ramir felt the tip of his dick tingling. Evea's swag excited him. She was a far cry from the sweet, homely, country girls from Florida that he was used to. Her aggressive confidence aroused him.

Evea led him to the kitchen where she had just finished preparing dinner. Ramir followed her like a trained seal.

"You up in here cookin' some good ole' food. Any man would love to come home to a beautiful shawty and a home cooked meal. Shit, I'm not leaving the house!"

Evea gave him a seductive laugh. "Ra, you just saying that."

Evea was in full character. This was business, but the pleasure was going to be all hers. Since the first night she laid eyes on him, she was feeling his swag. He was a rugged, pretty, country boy with two of the fullest lips made for two things: kissing and eating pussy. His lips were different, but his eyes are what really captivated Evea. His lashes were as long as hers, if not longer, and his eyes sparkled in the light.

Evea poured Ramir a glass of champagne. At first, he refused it, but she pulled him in with a bat of her eyes. "Come on. Have a drink. I hate to drink alone."

Ramir took the glass and began to sip. Even though his better judgement was warning him against his actions, the tingles coming from his tip were leading him in another direction. As Ramir finished up his second glass of champagne, Evea walked over to the stove and picked up a piece of her southern fried chicken. She took a bite and gestured for Ramir to try some. Fried chicken was one of his favorite dishes, but once again, he passed. Evea pouted as she stuck her index finger into the homemade mashed potatoes. Then she walked up to Ramir's face and placed her finger directly in his mouth. He could not control himself. He licked the potatoes off her finger slowly, while Evea stood face to face with him. Being almost eye level to him was different for her since she was used to sexing tall men.

Ramir instantly became rough with Evea. He spun her around to the back and began to bite on her neck. Evea had on a satin mini dress, which gave easy access to her curves. Ramir was in full glory! The feel of Evea's body excited him more than the visual. He played with her clit with just the right amount of pressure to bring her to a small orgasm. Evea's soft moans and dirty talk turned him on even more.

"You wanted this pussy all this time, didn't you? You

ready to fuck this pussy. Come on!"

Evea's sexy commands sent shockwaves up Ramir's spine. He dropped his pants and rammed deep into Evea's wet cush. She could feel every inch of Ramir's massive love stick. What he lacked in height, he made up for in inches. Evea cried out with each stroke. His dick played a magic trick as it disappeared deep inside her and then reappeared. Evea was fucking Ramir for revenge, but loving every second of their encounter. Ramir loved Evea's tight, wet spot. He forgot he was fucking somebody else's girl on the kitchen counter. As the strokes became more pleasurable to him, he pulled Evea's hair and watched the arch in her back deepen. Her moans and freaky talk sent Ramir over the edge.

"You 'bout to make dis dick nut. Oh shit, I feel it!"

Evea pushed away, confusing Ramir. She had climaxed several times, and now he was after his release.

"Shawty, what the fuck you doing?" Ramir asked out of breath.

Evea placed her finger on his lips. "Shhh!" she said while sliding to the kitchen floor. Ramir's eyes rolled in the back of his head. Evea was freaking him out. She slurped and sucked with much precision.

Between each deep throat, she moaned, "Mmmm, I want to taste all of you."

Ramir was no match for the knowledge Evea was giving him. "OHHHHHHHH, GOTDAMN, LIL MAMA! I'm 'bout to blow!"

Evea sucked hard, not wasting a drop of him. With Evea's

head buried deep in Ramir's lap and his loud screams, they did not hear the door that led from the garage into the house. There Adam stood watching his girl that he coveted so much deliver pleasure to another man in their kitchen.

"What the fuck?" Adam yelled. "Nigga, you done lost your country-ass mind! I hope you enjoyed that nut, 'cause it was ya last one! Evea, you dirty slut!"

"Fuck you, Adam! You filthy murderer! I know you killed my husband! How does it feel to have your heart ripped out like you did mine?"

Adam had finally heard the words that he dreaded for many years, and they were painful. Deciding that he and Evea were surely over, he headed toward his study and opened his top drawer to find his trusty handgun gone. He planned to shoot Ramir in cold blood in front of her. The empty drawer alarmed him.

Oh shit, this bitch done set me up! This nigga gonna kill me! Ramir was in shock. He had walked in on some movie-type shit. He knew Adam was hiding something, but banging the wife of the nigga he had killed was over the top even for Ramir.

Ramir attempted to exit the house, when Adam charged him from behind. He managed to break free and throw a hook that connected with Adam's left jaw. *Crack!* The sound echoed off of the walls, as Ramir's blow sent Adam flying across the room.

"Get out of here," Evea yelled to Ramir. "Now!"

Ramir took her advice and got out of the house as fast as

he could. As Adam charged at Evea, she quickly grabbed the would-be murder weapon for Ramir out of the solid wood drawer in the kitchen. The barrel of Adam's gun was pointed directly in his face, and the woman who he would die for now held his life in her hands.

*****

Love and the boys mounted up. G was so amped that he was finally going to be face to face with the nigga who had murdered Té that the excitement was killing him. The key players piled up in the squad's Black Expedition to head up the road for some closure.

As they were pulling out of the parking lot, a car speeding by almost hit them. They saw nothing but a blur in the rearview mirror. After inching up the street, they arrived in front of the house they believed to be Ramir's. Love had all of the lights out on the truck. They parked in front of someone else's driveway, and Love left the engine running. They could see the lights on and movement inside of the house. They could still see the truck that was delivered by the towing company earlier.

"Y'all ready, fellas?" Love asked. "Let's do this"

*****

Inside the house, Evea had turned in to a maniac. She held Adam at gunpoint and dialed on her cell phone with the other hand.

"What up, sis? Everything's ready out here." Tiff had just finished loading all of the cash Evea took out of Adam's safe into her car.

"Yeah, I'm almost done," Evea replied. "I need some help with an unruly guest."

Evea was speaking of Adam, but Tiff knew what she meant. Adam took advantage of Evea only having the gun steady with one hand and made his move. He side-swiped Evea, and her cell phone went flying.

"Evea! Evea! Evea!" Tiff yelled into the phone. All she could hear was struggling in the background. Tiff dropped her phone and took flight to assist her girl with her problem.

Booooom! The door that led to the guesthouse tumbled off of the hinges. Tiff arrived just in time. Adam was on top of Evea, and it was not looking good for her. He slapped her across her face with the gun he had stolen from her grasp. Tiff reached her side as she entered the house.

Bang! Bang! With no hesitation, Tiff busted her nine-millimeter. Adam fell to the floor on the same shoulder wounded from one of Tiff's shots. Holding her face, Evea rolled and spit in Adam's face as he lay on the ground holding his wound. Tiff stood over him, ready to end it all.

'Tiff, you've come too far in the plan. Just walk away," Evea pleaded with her. "Come on."

Tiff stood there staring at Adam with her gun still pointed at his head.

"Tiff, you made the call, didn't you? We have no time.

Now come on!" Evea pulled Tiff's arm.

She wanted to give Adam the same fate he had given her lover years ago. Deep down inside, though, she knew Evea's plan was better. Him losing her and all of his riches would kill him slowly.

Tiff and Evea ran out the back door, heading for Tiff's car that was filled of twenty million dollars.

*****

Love and the guys exited the truck when they saw flashing lights with no siren.

"Awww, shit," Love thought out loud. "Some of these white folks done called po-po on our asses."

The cars were headed directly at them. The SWAT, plainclothes, and uniformed cops followed each other to their destination. When they got to where Love had gotten out of the truck, they made a left turn into the driveway where he had been headed. The cops jumped out of their cars all at once, and in a matter of seconds, the entire place was surrounded. They went straight for the garage, as though they knew what they were looking for. Love, G, and company slid back inside the truck and watched as the police carried out credit card machines, boxes of guns, and other illegal items. For now, their search would have to wait until the heat was off the crib.

Chapter 16

Spring showers filled the air with the fragrance of watered flowers. Julie rolled over and admired the chocolate vision that lay before her. Love was still stretching to awaken from his peaceful sleep. Julie had placed a good screwing session on him the night before, and he fell fast asleep. Today was a new day, though. He was awake and ready to complete his mission.

Julie stepped down off of their platform bed onto the little step stool. The house that Love and Julie had leased for a few months was now beginning to feel more like a home. Julie tried to remind herself that their living arrangement was only temporary. She looked back at him, hoping their relationship was not temporary, as well.

After picking up her tooth cleaning kit from off of the side table, she entered the bathroom. Her steps quickened as she attempted to make it to the toilet. She passed the "his and her" sinks and sat the kit in front of the mirror. Like lightning, she made it to her destination and completed her mission. Julie exited the private toilet and made her way back to the sink.

While washing her hands, she whispered, "Blanca...now that's kind of catchy."

Julie had grown attached to the nickname in just a few short days. The name gave her a position and title. She liked that because she always felt like she was grabbing at straws trying to hold on to Love. She was pleased that his crew accepted her and hoped she could stick around.

When Julie turned on the water and lifted her head, she was met with Love's reflection in the mirror with hers and his morning erection on her bottom.

She jumped. "Baby, you scared me!"

"Now you know Daddy ain't gonna let nothing happen to his Blanca."

Love's statement incited a girlish smile. She was so attached to the name and smiled all over whenever he called her that, even though it only meant white in Spanish.

Love kissed Julie's rosy cheek and continued to the toilet. Julie gathered her floss, toothbrush, and pick to begin her morning oral hygiene routine. As she plucked, brushed, and gargled, Love continued to relieve himself. In between her obsessive teeth brushing frenzy, Julie looked up at the morning news to see what terrible things happened in the world while she was sleeping. That's when she almost choked on her saliva.

"Love!" She attempted to yell his name, but her sound was muffled due to a mouth full of water. Julie's coughing startled Love.

"J, you alright?"

"No, look at the TV!"

Love turned around to look at what was upsetting Julie so much.

"Turn it up!" she yelled.

Love said, "What? They just showing the same shit, killing and..."

Love's speech became baby-like as he struggled to form words. There Adam stood with his hands and feet shackled as they escorted him out of his upstate home with machine guns, credit cards, and thousands of stolen identities. Love could not believe his eyes!

"That's up the street from us! All this time that nigga been right under my nose!"

Love's cell phone was going off like crazy from other stunned and disappointed niggas in the crew. He did not have the words to express his emotions. Love and Julie sat in silence as the news media aired Adam's dirty laundry.

"Breaking news just in," the news anchor said. "Home in

an upscale community was raided late last night. An anonymous person called and tipped police off about a possible drug ring and identity theft operation. When the police arrived, they found Adamie Artez, also known as Andrew Adams, wounded and losing blood on the floor of the plush upstate home. Police confirmed that credit card machines, guns, and various other illegal items were seized from the house. This morning's story development has taken a turn for the worse for the suspect. Guns found in the home have several bodies on them. The police have issued a formal statement and Adamie Artez is charged with the murder of Donté Jordan, a victim slain in Philadelphia at a spring fling several years ago. The police are running ballistics on all of the firearms retrieved and say he may be charged with several other homicides." The anchorwoman then got close to the camera for dramatic affect. "Mystery caller, we all would like to thank you for aiding the police in the capture of another criminal with a gun! Join us at noon for more on this and other breaking stories."

*****

The news of Té's killer being caught quickly spread throughout the hood. Many of the guys Té grew up with were not pleased that Adam was going to get a cushy state house stay instead of getting handled by the streets. The idea of Adam having three hot meals and a cot was hard to swallow for those that knew and loved Té. The person that everyone was happy for was Té's mother. She could not rest since Té's murder. She still went to the door everyday and looked up and down the street, as if hoping her only son would return to her.

Mrs. Ethel May Jordan was a nice-looking sixty-year-old black woman. She was a sharp dresser and spared no expenses when it came to her jewelry. All the money Evea had sent her after Té's demise could not comfort her dying soul, though. Mrs. Jordan longed to feel close to her son again. One would think the news of Té's assassin being caught would give Mrs. Jordan's soul rest.

The morning the news announced Adam's capture, Mrs. Jordan sat in the living room with a cup of her favorite herbal tea at her side. She sipped the warm, calming substance in between deep breaths. When the news lady came on, all Mrs. Jordan heard was Té's name and something about the suspect being in custody. Her favorite mug went crashing to the floor and she soon followed. She cried out to God and wept until all of her mascara from the previous day was gone.

"Why did that monster have to take my baby?" she yelled.

Mr. Jordan almost slid down the steps as he attempted to reach his wife's side. He also had heard the news and could do nothing but kneel with his wife and hold her.

Mrs. Jordan cried for many reasons. The day Té was taken from her, she had become empty. The only thing that made her feel close to Té was Kayla, the seed of Té's loins, but she had disappeared, too. Mrs. Jordan often thought the lost of Té was just too much for Evea to bear, and that's why she ran off. Little did she know she had given Evea too much credit. She often had dreams of one day seeing Kayla and her favorite daughter-in-law again. With the news circulating, she hoped to have a reunion soon.

*****

Ramir awoke out of a deep slumber, hoping the events from the night before were just a dream. He rolled over with his head still spinning from all of the shots of Jack Daniel he had to help him clear his mind. He reached for his cell phone that lay on the floor next to his bed. His grasp was still weak from the massive headache he wore. As he made one final attempt to hold on the phone, he held it sideways to see what time it was. Ramir was concerned about the time because he had some business to take care of. He was meeting one of his homies from out of town around eight o'clock that evening to purchase some high-tech money counting machines. As he cleared his throat, he saw that the numbers on his BlackBerry read 6:15.

"Damn! I slept all day!" he said out loud. He had to move quickly, and that kind of pep he did not have.

Wanting to check out some SportsCenter, Ramir searched for the remote. He thought maybe a little Lebron James might get him motivated. He reached under his goose down pillows on his king-sized bed. The remote always got lost in the massive fluffy bed set that Ramir loved to wrap up in. He struggled and reached until finally he found his treasure. By that time, he was fully awake and agitated.

With one press of the power button, his 62-inch flat screen came alive. The television made people look as if they were sitting in his bedroom. Ramir's eyes leapt out of his head. Right there on the six o'clock news was a picture of Adam in cuffs being led to a police car as officers cleaned out his house. Ramir thought to himself, *This shit is bad...real bad.* He turned up the volume and heard the words that Evea had spoken to Adam the night before. It was confirmed. The crazy shit that Ramir was a part of at Adam's house was no dream! Adam was up for murder in the first degree and the bodies were piling up.

Ramir reached for his phone again and attempted to clear the screen. He had twenty new messages, and he did not have to guess what they were about.

Ramir dialed his voicemail and slowly put his code in.

The first message was from his out-of-town connect, who spoke in code.

Sup, Wawty, I know you probably still tied up, so just hit me ya address so we can do dinner at ya spot. I'm arriving in town early. Need to get wit'ya.

There was one message after another for Ramir to meet several members of his crew. Ramir sat straight up. His back was so stiff that he could not bend if he wanted to. He was glad no one in his crew knew his exact address. Like Jay-Z's classic hit song said, "Ya smile ain't matching ya tone." Each of his soldiers were hired hitmen. Ramir was well versed on the streets, and he got underestimated by a lot of city niggas because he was from a small town in Florida.

He quickly jumped to his feet and began throwing his belongings in a duffle bag. Ramir knew his minutes were numbered, and he was on his way back home. As he filled bag after bag with his important shit, he talked to himself out loud. "I don't believe this grimy nigga! He done put some bread on my head for some pussy. This shit is crazy!"

Ramir was Manny's first cousin on his dad side, and even though Manny was the leader of the crew and the one who placed Ramir next up to be Adam's partner, if he died, he knew money talked and niggas would kill their own mother for the right amount. He was not going to stick around to test their loyalty. So, Ramir gathered his bags and headed for his garage. He would have to bring the souped up Range Rover out for his long trip because he needed plenty of room for all his heat he was packing.

*****

Tiff laid poolside with the portable device on mute. She did not want to wake Evea. It had been a long night, and she wanted to let Evea rest up. Evea had been through so much those past few days, and Tiff was just happy to have her back.

They had drove half the night and ended up in Savannah, Georgia, at a wonderful condo that Tiff and Noah brought years ago. No one knew about the place but them, and they would travel all night just to wake up with each other surrounded by culture and beautiful craftsmanship. The condo was in downtown Savannah, and it overlooked the bridge and water stretched for miles. The 4,000 square-foot heaven was equipped with an indoor heated pool and spa. The hardwood floors were made of pure imported bamboo wood, and the twenty-foot high fireplace sat in the center of the open living room. Clearly, the handcrafted brick fireplace was the star of the show. It started from the floor and sent the eye on a wonderful voyage up to the twenty-foot cathedral ceilings.

Tiff watched the national news channel hoping to hear that Adam was dead. Just her luck, the nigga was on the screen walking with a lurch and his head hung low as the police escorted him from the hospital to the police car. Tiff had the television down so low that she could not hear a word. The volume did not matter to her, though. Evea had set Adam up good and took all of his money in the process.

Tiff cheered silently, controlling her tone. She had agreed with Evea not to kill him and to put his ass back in jail where she found him, but she did not say he would not meet his fate behind those walls. Tiff had a favor to call in. Adam had to die! She could not trust justice to be served.

Chapter 17

"What the fuck are you doing?!" Adam stood paralyzed while witnessing the horrific sight before him. Sex permeated through the air as sounds of physical pleasure bounced off of the wall. Adam was so enraged that his body became numb. He screamed louder, "Stop! Stop!"

They looked up stunned as their session was interrupted. Adam disappeared as he went to retrieve his weapon. Then he reappeared with his target in clear view. "Fuck this, muthafucka!" *BANG! BANG!*

Adam heard a loud screeching sound followed by a voice saying, "Restricted movement inmate roll call." He shot straight up in his bed, swung his feet around, and sat on the side of his bed. Adam was reminded that he was still behind bars and dreaming about the last time he saw Evea.

"Come on. Get y'all asses up and in view!" Officer Bruell yelled throughout the block as she stopped right in front of Adam's cell. "That means you, too, pretty boy." Officer Demy Bruell was 5'5" and built like a video vixen. She did not let her beauty define her. She was known as the toughest female officer in the prison.

With his head in his hands, Adam sat there still shaken from his dream. He felt like shit and could not believe he was back in the joint.

"Look, inmate, get ya ass up and get in line for roll call or you can line up in the hole's roll call for the next week!"

Adam looked up and caught a glimpse of her soft eyes. They seemed familiar, and he thought about Evea. He hated that she still held a space in his heart.

"Okay, officer, I don't want no problems," he said with a smirk as he struggled to get up from the bed.

He stared straight ahead as his mind raced about everything that had taken place. The love of his life tried to kill him and had sex with a nigga from his crew; his lawyer had not been returning his calls for the entire three weeks he was in lockup; and the prison food was making him ill.

Officer Bruell and Adam caught eyes, and he took his place in line. As Adam marveled at her sensuality, he recognized a softness that was easily overlooked by others due to her loud, harsh attitude. Officer Bruell's demeanor softened as she walked away from Adam. He may have been out of the loop in prison life, but he could sense weakness a mile away.

*****

"Goshen County Corrections Officer Steve Moore speaking!" Steve yelled to be sure the caller could hear him over all of the inmate chatter on the block.

"Hey, daddy, what's good?"

Steve sat straight up and began to breathe heavily.

"Hey, T, how you been?" Steve recognized Tiffany's voice immediately and began to get aroused at the mere thought of seeing her.

She smiled on the other end of the phone as she chuckled softly thinking about how excited Steve sounded. "I'm good. What about you?" Tiff hated that she had to participate in bullshit small talk with Steve.

They had a history, and it was no denying their chemistry. Steve and Tiff were hot and heavy years prior until she broke it off because Steve had become addicted to her. He was a deep chocolate treat with a naturally sculpted body that made Tiff melt into a puddle of pussy juices each time she saw his nakedness. Steve had one problem, though. He would become so sexually stimulated by Tiff and her freak show that he would have orgasms back to back before penetration. Tiff could not deal with the pre-ejaculation, limp dick syndrome, so she ended it. In exchange for her silence about his "problem", he vowed to help her with anything she needed.

Tiff kept their agreement for years, but was now calling him to collect.

"I'm better now that I hear your sweet voice," Steve responded in a seductive voice.

Tiff rolled her eyes and looked up at the ceiling in annoyance with his attempt to seduce her. "Yeah, my voice always made you feel better," Tiff said, playing along.

"That sweet voice was in my ear enough. How could it not make me feel better?"

Nigga, please, now you know ya dick don't stand a chance against all this! she thought to herself, but instead, she responded with, "Mmmm, I remember, too."

Tiff continued to pull him in with her phone-sex voice. "Daaaady, I need a favor." She let the "A" in daddy drag off of her tongue, arousing him even more.

"What do you need, T? Anything for you."

"Call me when you go on break so we can speak privately. I'll be waiting."

Steve sat back in the chair as his penis pulsated through his uniform. "I will hit you back in 'bout thirty minutes, Sweet T."

"Cool," Tiff replied with a sexy giggle. Then she hung up and continued to plan Adam's demise.

*****

Adam walked up behind an inmate who was yelling at his baby's momma on the pay phone.

"Damn, nigga, you got people waiting for the phone on

146

some bitch shit."

His fellow inmate turned around and began to lunge at him, but Officer Bruell rushed over and threw him against the wall. "You better calm down before you end up in the hole. Now take ya ass to ya cell to cool off."

Adam laughed as his plan worked since he was next up for the phone. Adam dialed the number and began his session.

"Yo, nigga."

"What up, my dude?" the person on the other end responded.

"Nothing, just this county shit. Did you ever get with Ra to take him out to lunch for his anniversary?" Adam was speaking in code about the hit he placed on Ramir. He named him as a snitch and state informant. That was not hard to believe since he was at Adam's house the night before Adam got knocked.

"Naw, I've been calling him and Boo went to check him out at the crib, but he was not at home. We think he went to visit family, so I sent his cousin down there to holla at him."

"Okay, nigga, tell him I said what's up when you see him."

"I got you, dawg. One."

Adam hung up the phone and headed back to his cell to plan his next move. His friend had just explained to him that Ramir had not been handled yet, but they were hot on his trail. Adam was not done, though. He had one more thing he had to handle to get him out and back on the streets.

He arrived at his cell and laid in his bottom bunk. He thought about Officer Bruell and how he could get her on his team. He needed access to his slimy-ass lawyer, and he had used all of his phone time. Besides, he was starting to believe his lawyer was screening his calls from the prison, and he needed an outside line.

*****

Joseph Miller, Esq. sat at his oversized oak desk looking through some files. He was a tall older gentleman with salt and pepper hair. He looked through the rolodex as he retrieved the phone number to the county prison. He called to alert the social worker that he would be in to see his client, and explained that depending on how things went, he may need counseling.

After hanging up, Mr. Miller headed out of his center city office. As he stood waiting for his car from the valet, he thought about the hour drive ahead of him and the possible outcome.

*****

Adam was fresh out of ideas when he accepted the fact that he would need more time to study Officer Bruell if he would get her on his team. As he thought about her face, body, and smell, he became aroused. Adam lay in his bed in full glory with his eyes closed. He felt as if she was right in the cell with him as her perfume became more vivid. He got deeper into his fantasy until he heard, "Adamie, let's go. You have a visitor."

He jumped up, hard on in plain view as he attempted to gather himself. There in his door stood Officer Bruell.

Damn, how long has she been standing there? he said to himself. He prepared to be searched before leaving his block, but he held on to his fantasy.

Chapter 18

The light glared into the window of the dim living room. Kayla rolled over to cover her face with the throw that she had fallen asleep on. While clearing her throat, she looked around for the TV remote. She barely had a voice due to yelling and crying night after night. She even stopped taking Jason's calls and going outside period. Evea had called her hundreds of times and all she could do was reach her mother. Kayla felt betrayed and empty. Her rage was increasing as the days continued. She felt as if she had lost both parents. The strong mother that she once looked up to had vanished, and she was left with disappointment and disgust in her place. Kayla thought of ways she could get Adam, but he was in jail and out of her grasp.

Kayla reached the remote and turned it on to see the time. It was early afternoon, and her grandmother had been calling her to get up and get going on her chores and school project for a few hours. Finally, Kayla peeled herself off of the sofa and headed for her bathroom. She convinced herself that she was going to have a good day and stop being so depressed. After making it to her bathroom, she started her shower water, and as she checked the temperature, her cell phone blared from her purse. She recognized the ringtone and decided to be among the living.

"Hey, baby," she answered.

"Sweetheart, what's good with you? I been worried sick. Are you cool?"

"I'm better now that I hear your voice." Kayla spoke as if she did not shut him out for weeks at school and on the phone.

"Well, I'm glad to hear your voice, too, sexy." Jason was so smitten with Kayla, and the truth was he would have waited as long as she needed him to just to get back in her presence. "I want to see you today. We can do anything you like. You name it!"

Kayla paused and then replied, "I'm free, but I have to do my chores and start this project. Then we can roll."

"See you later, sexy girl."

Kayla smiled, which was something she hadn't done in a while. "Okay. Love you, boy!"

*****

Evea lay across her bed looking at all of the things that reminded her of her life with the man who killed her husband. She hadn't been back at the house since the FEDS ransacked the place weeks prior. She sobbed uncontrollably, hating herself for being so stupid. She realized that her stupid affair affected many people's lives, and now she could not even bear to live with the hurt of losing her daughter.

Tiff entered the bedroom and rubbed Evea's head. She tried to take the pain away, but Evea was too far gone. She hated that she could not be there for Kayla and missed her husband tremendously. The hole in her heart had increased in size, and she could not close it despite her efforts. Tiff was happy that her best friend was back in her life, but hated that she could not help her heal. After Tiff cued Evea in on the plan to get rid of Adam for good, that seemed to bring her some peace, but she could not wait until the plan unfolded.

Chapter 19

The sun seemed to be a little brighter as Boo looked up and saw the sign "Welcome to Florida". He stopped at the gas station to use the restroom and gather some supplies.

He planned on laying low until nightfall when Ramir would have to get dealt with once and for all.

Boo continued his journey after his pit stop and set up camp at Ramir's family's house. He slid down deep in the seat of his black Impala, listening to Plies' "Murkin' Season" to get hype for his impending task. People were coming and going in and out of the home, but there was no sign of Ramir anywhere.

Nightfall came, and it was time for him to take action. Boo

watched Ramir's brother and girlfriend exit the house, and she got into her car, kissed him, and drove off. Boo checked his heat, a glock nine, a .45, and Desert Eagle with hollow-tip bullets. Boo then exited the Impala, leaving his door open for a quick getaway. While pulling his black ski mask down to hide his identity, Boo moved swiftly as the shadows from the palm trees swayed to and fro. Just as Ramir's brother reached the front door, Boo was on his back with the .45 urging him on.

"Nigga, keep moving!" Boo said with a stern tone. "Turn around and I'ma blow ya face off!"

Ramir's brother continued to move and follow his request as he put one hand up. Once inside, Boo wasted no time. He hit Ramir's brother with the butt of the gun while pointing the Desert Eagle at all who were present.

"Hit the floor, niggas! Where is that snitching sack of shit Ramir?!"

Everyone remained silent.

BANG! BANG! "Warning shot, niggas!"

A female that was present screamed in horror, "We don't know where he is! Please don't hurt my babies!"

Boo looked at her and laughed. "Bitch, you better start talking if you want any of y'all to live."

"NNNNNOOOOOOOOOOO! Please! We don't know!"

Ramir's brother, who was just waking up from the nap that Boo had given him, said, "Look, nigga, we don't know where my brother is. He's been gone from down here for a long while, ya heard me!"

Boo was growing agitated with their hick talk and bitching. So, he aimed and shot. *BANG! BANG! BANG!*

"Give him that message when you see him!" Boo shot Ramir's brother in the leg and arm, then shot his baby's mother in the foot. He turned to run out, then sped off and pulled in to a secluded area a few miles up the road.

"Yo, my nigga, dude was nowhere to be found. No one has seen him, and I believe them 'cause I left a present for them all and they still stuck to their stoooory." Boo's last word was slurred and unclear. The phone dropped to the floor, leaving his partner on the other end confused.

"Yo, nigga, you there? What's going on?"

Boo gave no response. All that could be heard was loud gurgling. Blood sprayed everywhere as the slit in his neck ushered him to the other side. He had just met Radeah, Ramir's twin sister, and she was the last image he saw in his rearview mirror.

*****

Adam's search before leaving the block was complete. He gathered his clothes and adjusted himself. Officer Bruell gestured for him to follow her as she walked like she had on heels and fishnet pantyhose...sexy and confident. Adam stared at her ass like he was studying for a test. She stopped at the officer's desk to sign him out before taking him to visitation. Adam's stare was broken.

"Follow me, Mr. Artez."

Adam obeyed her command, but thought to himself, *Who the hell wants me? I didn't even put in for any visitations. What if it's Evea? Yeah, she's coming back begging.* He walked down three long corridors surrounded by cinderblock beige walls. When Adam arrived at the private visitation room, his eyes lit up.

After Adam approached the rectangular metal table that was anchored to the floor, an arm reached over the table in a gesture of a handshake. Adam looked at Mr. Miller up and down and sat in the chair opposite him. Mr. Miller, who was visibly insulted, gestured to the guard to wait on the outside of the room. Then they sat opposite sides of the table surrounded by silence.

Adam continued to look into his hands attempting to hold all the emotion inside that if he let go would get him another case. Mr. Miller awkwardly cleared his throat and looked up at the window in the center of the aluminum door. He was checking to be sure the guard was in place. Mr. Miller did not know Adam to be a violent man, but the news he would deliver had the potential to send the most humble man into frenzy. Adam looked across the table as Mr. Miller fumbled with his important papers. Finally, Adam broke the silence.

"What pathetic excuse do you have for leaving me in this hellhole for three weeks and not returning my calls?!"

Mr. Miller looked as if he swallowed a beach ball. "Adamie, listen, I needed time to get things in order. You have to understand I was working on your behalf."

"Nigga, please!" Adam yelled as his fist met the tabletop.

"You expect me to believe that shit. You have the keys to my secure locker at the club and access to my legal account for the shop, so what the fuck am I still doing in this place? Your money-hungry ass thought you was gonna play me and get away with it!" Adam went on and on, not giving Mr. Miller the opportunity to answer any of his questions. Mr. Miller spoke in a timid voice. He was apprehensive (to say the least) about giving him the news.

"Adamie…"

"Don't call my name with that timid shit. You ain't my girl!"

Mr. Miller's demeanor went from concerned to agitated. "Look, ADAM!"

Adam stopped and gave his full attention.

"I was not trying to steal shit from you. Quite frankly, I have been doing the total opposite. I spent the past three weeks searching for a way to fix up your shit so I didn't have to visit you in this hellhole with this fucked-up news!"

"Miller, what the hell are you talking about?" Adam demanded.

"As soon as I saw your picture on the news, I began to get our defense together. When I arrived at the club and went into the locker room where the private lockers were located to take out my retainer and get bail money, what I saw was devastating. The walk-in locker was completely empty. All that remained was this letter with your name written in blood!"

Adam's stomach turned, and he felt like he was going to

let it go any minute.

"So you telling me that all my fucking money is gone?! six million dollars vanished!" Adam stood to his feet with rage in his eyes. "How do I know you ain't take my shit for yourself?"

As Adam walked closer to him, the guard entered the room with his walkie-talkie out ready to call for swat. "Inmate Artez, take a seat or go back to you cell!"

After Adam sat back in his seat, Mr. Miller assured the officer that he was okay. "Here's the letter."

Mr. Miller handed the pink envelope to Adam with an unsteady hand. "What the fuck is this?"

"It's the letter I told you about."

"What type of gay shit is this?" Adam took the envelope, which had a familiar smell. He sat back in the chair with the envelope in his hands under the table as he slid it in his sleeve.

"Adam, it gets worse. I checked on your accounts for the shop and and other businesses. All of the legal accounts for them are all empty."

"So you telling me that them damn FEDS got all my shit on lock? How did they even know about the detailing shops?"

"I was curious about the same thing. So, I made some calls and did some research. The FEDS did not have any record of those accounts in any of their paperwork. So, I called Evea to get her to do some research on the business accounts, and she was anything but polite."

Adam stood up again, and this time, he was not sitting down! "Muthafucka, you ain't shit! If your stupid ass would have done your job, all of my money would not be gone! That

160

bitch wouldn't have had time to fuck me over!" Adam yelled as he lunged across the table, now holding Mr. Miller's life in his hands as he chocked him with all of his might.

The officer jumped on his back and attempted to remove his hands from the lawyer's neck, but with no luck.

"Code blue in visitation room sixteen!" the officer yelled in his radio.

Adam continued to take all of his frustration out on Mr. Miller as he banged his head on the floor. Adam heard the loud footsteps of backup as the officers marched to the visitation area. He released his grip, dropped Mr. Miller, and stood up with his hands above his head. The officers entered the area swinging clubs and yelling, "Get down!" After shackling Adam, they dragged him down the corridors where he would be confined to his cell until his administrative hearing.

*****

Tiff rode up the expressway while attempting to connect her call to the wireless headset. "Bitch, hold on. You talking to the air. I'm not trying to get pulled over by these head crackers out here."

Peaches continued to go on and on about their meeting later, while Tiff struggled to get her headset to stay on. "Tiff, what the hell are you doing?"

"Hello…hello…Bitch, I told you to hold on, and you just can't stop talking."

"Girl, I didn't hear you with all the rumbling in your

phone!" Tiff finally had her headset on properly. "Like I was saying, I can't wait to see Evea. I cannot believe that sheisty bastard had her fooled all this time. But, fuck him. Tonight, we celebrate life!"

"Damn right! I have to get something to wear. I'm on my way back to town now. I just left Evea, and she was finally getting herself together and was able to stop crying long enough to plan her outfit."

"Now you know fashion could always snap her ass out of anything."

They both laughed.

Beep! "Hold on! That's my other line. Did your ass hear that?" Tiff teased as she clicked over to her call waiting. "Hello."

"Hey, sexy, are you ready to tell me how I can help you?"

Tiff paused and then recognized the voice. "Hey, daddy, are you ready for this? I have a question first."

"Yes, always ready for you!"

"Do you have an inmate in the jail named Adamie Artez? Or should I say, I need you to find out what block he's on…"

Steve interrupted her. I don't have to find out. I know what block he's on if we're talking about the same person. I did some overtime on his block last night."

Tiff listened intensely. "Well, how does he look?" Tiff was so into the conversation with Steve that she let Peaches hang up without warning.

Steve cleared his throat and continued. "He's a tall, brown skin, pretty-looking muthafucka."

"That's our man." Tiff continued to explain her situation and her need for Steve's services. After listening to Tiff's plan, Steve signed on as a willing participant in the hunt for Adam!

Back at the jail...

Adam made it back to his cell ushered by two large, overly aggressive officers. One of the tall bald-headed officers ordered him to stand still while he removed his shackles.

"Listen, asshole. I'm not that pussy-ass lawyer of yours. I will fuck you completely up! You lucky his bitch ass refused to press charges, claiming you were under distress! He was the fuck delirious after that choking you put on him, but remember I ain't him! Now, get ya bitch ass in the cell."

The officer pushed Adam so hard that he fell and hit his head on the wall.

"Damn, man, you a'ight?" Adam's cellie asked.

Fuming with anger, Adam snatched away. "I'm fine, nigga!" He got up and dusted his jumper off as the two oversized prison emergency response officers walked away in laughter.

Adam had so many thoughts running through his mind. He went over all the people that knew about his locker in the club, but he kept coming up with only him and Mr. Miller. Not even Evea knew anything about his dirty money. Adam traced his steps and thought until he had a headache.

"Shit! This is fucked up!" Adam let out a loud roar. His mind raced some more as he banged his fist on the bed. As he banged harder, the tip of the pink envelope peaked out of his sleeve. Adam's eyes lit up. "Oh shit! I almost forgot."

Adam's cellie looked at him like he was going mad as he talked to himself. Adam settled in to his bed and cracked open the mysterious letter.

He sniffed the envelope again to put his finger on the smell. Then he unfolded the lined paper, and his eyes danced along each red line.

Dear Adamie,

I don't even know if I should call you that. Is that even your real name? You fooled me; no, you deceived me with selfish gain in mind. I gave myself to you, a person who was not worthy of any of my time let alone my love, my treasure. You preyed on me like a wolf on a lamb, taking from me that which I adored more than you...more than life. My beloved husband! You left a hole in my heart so big that it could never be filled, not even by your icy hot love. So, I guess by now you know who I am. I hate you! I hate that you ever experienced the essence of me. But, for now, revenge will have to do. Yes, I have taken from you all that you hold dear in this world...all of your money and most of all, my love! A love you were willing to steal by taking a life. I hope you know all that you own is gone. Have fun trying to beat all of your charges with a public defender. Finally, I'm glad you're back where you belong and where I should have left your no-good ass. Cycle complete...360 degrees of Karma!

Lovingly,
MRS. Jordan

PS. I hope you liked the scratch and sniff envelope! Be sure to lick the envelope, because that's the last time you will smell or taste my sweet pussy. Goodbye forever.

Adam lay there gritting his teeth and fighting back the tears. His world was crumbling down, and he had no idea how to fix it. He had to go hard and call his crew for support.

*****

On the other side of the wall...

The moon was flickering off of the black S-Type Jaguar. G sat back in his chair as the butter soft, heather grey leather consumed his big frame. Peaches sat on the passenger side applying her lip gloss. She could tell G was in deep thought. She broke the silence with her bubbly personality.

"Hey, baby, guess what I'm thinking about right now?"

He continued to look forward as he came to a red light. "I don't know, sweetie. What?"

"I'm thinking about our session earlier when you held me up on your shoulders and gave me the best head in my life. Mmmm, I'm still tingling!"

G looked at Peaches with a pleasantly surprised look. He knew Peaches' sexy side, but this was a little out of character. Peaches waited for a response, but all she received was a smile.

"G, what's wrong with you? What's on your mind?"

"Look, babe, I can't stop thinking about Evea being with that nigga all these years since my homie's murder. That shit got me fucked up. She's like family to me!"

"I know. It is a little crazy, but everybody is so happy

about Evea being back. You don't understand. That dirty bastard had her thinking that people were after her and Kayla and he needed to protect them. That nigga gonna get what he deserves. Trust that!" Peaches rubbed G's hand to soothe him. "Let's try to enjoy our outing before Evea's get-together later.

*****

Tiff was singing and running her bathwater as she went over her brilliant plan in her head. Adam was going down and she loved it. She felt bad that she did not include Evea in her plan. She smiled at the thought of Evea being satisfied at the surprise revenge she had planned.

Hearing a thump downstairs and then footsteps, Tiff reached for her lady nine that lay on the counter of her state-of-the-art bathroom. She stood in her bathroom in all of her glory with the gun pointed at the door. The bedroom door opened and she cocked back.

"Don't take another step, nigga!" she yelled.

When Noah turned the corner, Tiff let out a sigh of relief. He took her hand with the gun in it and pointed it to the floor. "Damn, shawty, you a bad bitch. That's why you my baby!"

They both laughed.

"It wouldn't be funny if I had put some hot shit in ya ass, now would it? How many times have I told you to call me when you're coming in the house? I can't hear everything in this big-ass house."

"You sure heard my ass," Noah teased.

166

"Oh shit, Noah, my bath water!" Tiff directed her attention to the bath.

"I'm getting all smooth and sexy for our girls' meeting with Evea. We will see y'all boys after we do the girl thing."

Noah stood there in his classic Guess jeans, a button-up shirt, and classic ¾-length Timberlands...straight 1990's hustler style. Noah was rugged but sexy and loved throwback gear.

When Tiff bent over to cut off the faucet, Noah lost his train of thought as he was graced with a full back-shot view. "Damn, T, that ass getting fatter each day!"

Tiffany smiled as she gestured for him to join her in the tub. After snatching off his clothes like he had on basketball warm-ups, he hurried to the tub where his pleasure awaited. Noah slid one foot at a time in the medium hot water.

Noticing his sensitivity to the temperature, Tiff commented, "I like my water like I like my men...hot and smooth."

Noah sat opposite Tiff in their two-person garden tub. He slid his right hand under the water and grabbed her left butt cheek to pull her onto his lap. Tiff let out a big sigh as she mounted his full manhood. Placing her hands behind her, she went up and down on his tip while he played with her clit just right. Before Noah could tug at her clit once more, Tiff's legs began to shake, and she squirted white hot all on him. Noah was in a giving mood and he loved to make Tiff cum until she was docile.

He stood up and ushered Tiff's lower body above her head

while she still had her hands on the base of the tub. Noah held Tiff up with her legs spread wide while she remained in a handstand. Then he licked her hot spot slowly from front to back until she screamed, finally having an orgasm so hard that she had tears streaming down her face.

"Oh...oh...oh, baby! I'm cuming again. Please stooooooop! Mmmmmmmmmmmm."

Noah's dick grew in size. Just when Tiff lay in the tub trying to catch her breath while tingling all over, he picked her up, faced her toward the wall, and dove deep into her wetness, ready for blast off.

*****

Evea blazed up the expressway with the top down on her brand-new emerald green Aston Martin, her latest gift to herself with Adam's money she knew nothing about. She blasted her state-of-the-art stereo singing along with all of the words to her and Té's song from back in the day, "You're All I Need" by Mary J. Blige and Method Man. Music and shopping always made Evea feel better. She thought about her love lost and missed his presence even more. She was running late but felt she owed it to Té to remember him daily, which was something she struggled with when she was with Adam. When Evea saw the city lights that she had not laid eyes on in years, she got a sparkle of excitement in her stomach. She was in Philly; she was home.

Tiff arrived at The Chart House Restaurant on Delaware

Avenue in the heart of the city. She pulled up to the valet in her powder pink BMW two-seater with cream leather seats. As she exited the car, her style overshadowed her stylish ride. She was elegant in her strapless black Chanel mini-dress and cream studded 5-inch heels as she rounded off her look with an ocean-blue envelope clutch.

Tiff entered the restaurant and was led to their private area where the rest of the girls sat there waiting. Plumie, Kiwi, and Peaches were all excited to see Evea and catch up on lost time. They shared tears of joy and had girl talk until she arrived. The crew reminisced on how many years they had been friends and acknowledged Evea's important part in all of their lives.

As the girls' tears of joy turned to loud laughter, Peaches spotted their guest of honor. Tears streamed down her face as Evea approached the table. She was radiant. Her hair was jet black in curly, long layers. Evea's style was still impeccable. She wore a one-of-a-kind pink and burgundy lace and tulle halter dress that fell right above the knee. She had on 4-inch silver strappy Kenneth Cole stilettos and carried an understated jeweled wristlet. When Evea spotted the girls, the emotions took over, and they all rushed her and stood in the middle of the restaurant in a group hug.

Tiff broke up the hug and raised her voice saying, "No more tears, bitches. My sister is home. So, let the drinks flow and the bullshit begin!"

Everyone raised their glasses, and Tiff gestured for the waiter to pour Evea some champagne. The busy patrons focused their attention toward the secluded party in the corner of the restaurant as the party began.

*****

G, Love, Corn, Jay-Roc, Noah, and their newest crew member sat and discussed business plans before they joined the girls.

"Listen, my man here has given us a lot of inside information, and we gonna use this to screw that nut-ass nigga. My man will not lie in his grave in vain. Tiff explained the whole plan to me, and I shared the shit with all of y'all. This shit has to be done exactly like we discussed in order to get this nigga back for good."

Noah spoke directly to his crew and was careful with what he said in front of the newcomer that Love and G endorsed.

Jay exploded. "This shit is one thing I can't wait for, but remember, don't mention shit to Evea tonight. This is a joyous celebration, and no matter what y'all think of her, remember Té loved her. So, that makes her important!"

Noah responded, "I agree, and remember, Evea don't know about the plan. So keep ya mouths shut, niggas! If you can't hold ya liquor, then don't drink shit."

*****

Adam was boiling inside. He never could imagine feeling this much hatred for Evea in his life. He blamed her for everything and vowed to get even with her. He read her letter over and over as he thought of what and who he could use to get her back. He needed a phone call, and he needed it badly in order to put his plan in motion. He had one problem, though. He was confined to his cell until the next day, so his contact would have to wait.

Officer Steve entered the block and gave his colleagues a handshake as he went inside the officer's booth. Steve made small talk as he cased the joint out to see where Adam was. He did not see him anywhere. Hearing his fellow officers talking about an inmate who had chocked out his lawyer, Steve joined the conversation.

"Damn, man, what did I miss on my break?"

"That new nigga in cell fourteen, Adamie Artez, went off on his lawyer. Now he won't be out until tomorrow for his hearing."

"Wow," Steve said as he put his plan together in his head. "I'm gonna head to master control. I been in this bitch since this morning."

The two officers gave Officer Steve some dap, and he exited the block.

*****

Evea and the girls were on their fifth round as they sang and laughed about their years of escapades. Evea came to dinner feeling heavy and empty without the love of her life. Being in the company of good friends, food, and drinks had lifted her spirits and made her thank God for having such wonderful girls in her life. She wondered how she made it without them.

The celebration continued until Tiff got a call from Noah alerting her that they were outside. Tiff informed the girls that the boys would soon be inside. Evea was excited, but was anxious about how the men would respond to her now that they knew the truth about Adam. So, she quickly took two Patrón shots to the head to try to calm her nerves.

The boys walked in looking good enough to eat and turning heads as they walked by. They all were familiar, but one of them looked misplaced. Evea almost choked on her drink. Kiwi and Plumie gave a second look at the new guy as Evea sat there in shock.

"Hey, E," Noah said, breaking the ice as he embraced her like he always did.

G stood there frozen in time in the back of the line waiting to get his hug, as well. Evea looked over Noah's shoulder, and she and G locked eyes. She thought her husband was staring her in the face, and her emotions overtook her. Noah moved to the side, and G stood in front of her with his arms outstretched.

Crying, Evea fell into his arms, saying, "Welcome home, brother. Welcome home."

Once she stepped back, the men ordered another round. They stood up with glasses raised and saluted Evea, who swallowed her drink down in one gulp and headed for the door in tears.

Chapter 20

The lyrics to "I'm So Hood" blasted from Ramir's phone, playing the same verse over and over. He rolled over in an unfamiliar room that was plush and equipped with everything. He searched through the strange sheets to find out where his phone was hiding.

"What it do?" he said in a scratchy southern voice.

The voice on the other end yelled, "Nigga, where the fuck you at? We about to make a move, and if you not here by the time we planned, then the deal is off and you back on our hit list, too!"

"Dude, you gotta calm down on the threats. Breathe easy.

I'm finna to come. I will be on time."

"You better be!"

Ramir looked over at the sexy creature as he exited the bed. He could not believe the connection he felt with her. Maybe it was the sex or the damsel in distress thing, but either way, he wanted to know more.

Evea rolled over and curled up in her down comforter, trying to lay her head a certain way to get rid of her hangover headache. Her eyelids struggled to open, and when they finally defeated gravity, she could not believe her eyes. The comforter that she was wrapped up in was not her own, and the bedroom, while stylish, was far from her sanctuary. She looked up over the covers and caught a glimpse of Ramir's sexy, naked body coming out of what looked like the bathroom.

"Morning, sleepyhead," Ramir said in a playful manner.

"What the hell is going on? How…where am I?"

"You're at my newly purchased condo about one hour outside of Philly."

"What?! This shit is crazy. How did I get here?"

Ramir stopped putting his pants on and turned to face Evea. "The short version is all I have time for, shawty. You left our dinner all emotional and drunk. I followed you to make sure you would get home okay and wound up leaving my car parked about an half hour from here in order to take your car because you stopped at a gas station and stumbled to the pump."

"Okay, but why am I here instead of home?"

"You was freaky as shit in the car and wanted to come to

the closest spot for some humpin'. I thought you were just drunk and planned on bringing you here to sober up, but you put it on me and I couldn't resist."

Evea sat listening while images of their amazing night played in her head. *I thought I had a wet dream, but that shit was real,* she thought to herself. She could not get his beautiful dick out of her mind and the way he touched her...she was sure it was a dream.

"Shawty, I gotta blow, so I will catch you lata'. You mo' than welcome to lay low here until you feel betta. I got some business to handle." Ramir could speak in the up north slang, but he used his broken English and southern slang when he felt comfortable with someone.

Ramir walked over, gave Evea a kiss on the cheek, and headed for the door. Evea retrieved her cell phone and cleared her message screen. After getting comfortable, she dialed Tiff's number.

*****

Ramir bumped his southern favorite Plies all the way to the meeting spot. Since his car was still parked at the gas station, he drove his Range Rover. He thought about what he had signed up for and hated that he had to become a snitch. He knew it had to be done once his sister gave him the call about his rogue crew member, Boo.

"Fuck it! That nigga Adam is like cancer, and he has infected the whole operation. He and they have to go!" Ramir spoke aloud to himself.

When Ramir arrived at the spot, everybody was in place. They followed him and trusted his knowledge about each spot. He encouraged them to hit them by day because that was when they were most vulnerable. They pulled on their hoodies and started toward the first house with force.

The back door swung open, and Love entered the house blazing two .45 caliber handguns, hitting all of his targets. The rest of the boys came up from the basement and through the front door. They all went to work without any instruction. Their movement was that of a perfectly choreographed dance. They left no witnesses and took over five hundred thousand dollars from each house in money and merchandise. By 4:00 p.m., they had hit each of Adam's houses, killing and robbing them blind. G and Love were glad Ramir joined forces with them after Love ran into him on his way out of town.

Evea's attempts to reach Tiff were unsuccessful. She was in no condition to be getting involved with anyone, and she needed to speak to Tiff immediately. While taking a break from hunting Tiff down, she decided to listen to her messages. She had several messages from the girls worried about how she made out. Tiff left a message that reminded Evea of a necessary outing they had planned.

"Hey, E, it's me. I know you feel fucked up right now and seeing all of them brought back a lot of memories that you have suppressed for so long. No more hiding, E. It's time to get closure. You need to go to Té's grave like we planned so you can have your last talk with him. Please call me. I know

Té has forgiven you, and it's time to forgive yourself."

Evea's eyes filled up with tears that she was sick of crying. Tiff was right, and Evea planned on meeting her at the grave like she promised.

Evea got up out of the bed, wrote Ramir a note, and headed home to take her life back.

*****

Adam awoke to the sounds of a jungle, people yelling and officers waking inmates who needed meds and had appointments. Adam got up and participated in his morning ritual. He kept Evea's letter under his pillow for motivation to go all the way. When Officer Bruell stopped in front of his cell to do a routine cell check, Adam took advantage of her soft spot for him.

"Good morning, Officer Bruell," Adam said with a sexy smile and his curly black hair perfectly groomed.

"Good afternoon, Inmate Artez. You missed morning by several hours."

Time seemed to fade away inside the jail. Adam forgot he had taken a few naps throughout the day. "I need to get my phone call for the day. I didn't have one yet."

She stood there staring at his physique. "That's because you on the hearing list, and you have to get it after your hearing."

Adam started to feel defeated and thought to himself that he may have misread her vibes.

Officer Bruell continued, "But since you're so cute, I will make an exception for you."

Adam's eyes lit up like fireworks. She opened his cell and off he went to the phone. He needed to call his connect to put his plan to get his money back in motion. Once at the payphone, Adam dialed Kyle's cell number. Kyle was his second in command since Ramir was gone and he was in jail. Plus, he was the only one Adam could trust to handle business as ordered.

The phone rang over and over, and his answering machine wasn't picking up. Growing upset, Adam called house after house, cell phone after cell phone, but no one was answering. He wanted to put his crew on Kayla to get Evea to pay ransom. He had it planned out to where she would give him his money back and he would be able to pay for a lawyer.

"Inmate Artez, time for hearing," the officer called throughout the block.

Adam made his way to the front of the block where he needed to be searched before leaving. He made long strides, and before he knew it, a tall, black, burly inmate bumped into him.

"Nigga, watch where you going, pretty boy!" he said as he pushed him to the floor.

Adam jumped up and began swinging wild punches at him as they connected and wrestled around until they both ended up on the floor again. A long metal shank fell and made a loud clinking sound. The block went into a loud roar as the officers attempted to break it up. Adam was carried away, and the mystery inmate was shackled and subdued. The officers escorted Adam off of the block.

He was sure he still had to go to his hearing, when he was carted past the hearing room and thrown in the hole (administrative segregation). The big black guy was taken to the hole, as well, and the large shank was bagged for evidence. The officers that broke up the fight arrived at the hearing and explained that they retrieved a shank as a result of Adam's scuffle on the block a few minutes prior.

Lieutenant Knight, who was very agitated by this behavior, looked over his glasses and said, "So you mean to tell me this inmate was on trial for assault on his lawyer, and he engaged in a fight with a weapon on the way to my hearing room! He has to go! Effective immediately! I do not need any hot-headed troublemakers on my watch!"

Lieutenant Knight was a veteran in the prison system and had a lot riding on his new position. He was not about to keep an unruly inmate around and have him look like a fool. The officers exited his office, and Lieutenant Knight leaned back in his chair and thought to himself how to get Adam out of his hair.

*****

Evea pulled up in her driveway with memories of her and Adam still fresh in her mind. As she approached the house, she felt a profound sadness. Evea entered the kitchen and laid her keys on the counter. She got the tea kettle out and began to run water. That's when she heard footsteps in the background and hoped she was not in any danger.

She slid to the island anchored in the center of the kitchen and reached for the concealed weapon under the countertop. When she turned around, there stood Kayla with concerned eyes. Evea dropped the gun and ran to hug her daughter. This was an overdue homecoming.

Chapter 21

Adam lay in his dark cell staring at the ceiling with nothing but boxers on and a mattress without sheets. The days seemed to melt away, night merging with day and vice versa. Adam thought of Evea often. He was furious with her for trying to destroy him, but he yearned for her smell and touch. He closed his eyes, and there she stood staring at him with her beautiful eyes. She smiled at him, and he reached out to touch her but reached for the plain air.

He sat up in frustration, feeling broken. His sadness turned in to anger as he stood up and punched the wall. Adam felt like a trapped, wounded animal, and spending days in the hole did not help. Being incarcerated was a problem in itself, but spending time in the hole where there was no movement happening, no yard time, or no contact with others was a slow death.

Adam turned to walk to the other side of his cell when he heard keys jingling. It was the officer unlocking his cell, and he was more than relieved to get out of that small-ass space.

*****

The light peaked through the half cracked shade, creating a stream of light that shone directly on the bed. *Ring...ring...ring...ring.* The phone continued to chime as Evea struggled to find the cordless phone.

"Where the hell is that damn thing?" Evea yelled to the top of her lungs.

Whoever was calling really needed to get in touch with her because they hung up and called back to back. Finally, it stopped ringing, but she continued to search just in case they called again. She lifted the covers off of Kayla to see if she was laying on it. As she placed the covers back on her, Trina's classic "Baddest Bitch" blared from her cell phone. Evea reached over to the nightstand feeling awkward in her own bedroom. She had not stayed in her home since that night Adam was taken away.

"Hello," Evea answered out of breath.

"Damn, bitch, where you been? I have not seen or talked to you since the night of the party. You okay?"

"And good morning to you, too, Tiff! I'm fine...well, as

fine as I can be these days," Evea replied.

"Where the hell did you go when you stormed out of the restaurant? What the hell was that about? You acted like you saw a ghost!"

Evea took a deep breath. "Girl, I saw two ghosts and a fucking reindeer."

They both started to laugh. Evea cleared her throat as she walked out of the room from where Kayla was sleeping.

"Listen, I called you yesterday morning when I woke up in Ramir's bed!"

"What? Who the fuck is Ramir and how you get in his bed?" Tiff asked. "Was it on some date rape shit? 'Cause I'm ready to blast a nigga. I ain't cock my gun back in a while!"

"Girl, calm the hell down. No! Ramir, known as Ra, is the dude that Adam brought home and who now is hanging with Noah and the boys."

"Oh, that's the dude you met when Adam's ass was shot that night?"

"Yes. He kinda caught me giving him head the night we put our plan in place to fuck him up."

Tiff sat straight up in her seat. "You ain't shit! You left that detail of that night out! That nigga is sexy! Here I am scoping him for a possible side john since he's new and all, and you done got the goods!" Tiff said as she laughed in between words.

"Tiff, focus! He followed me to be sure I got home safely, and I ended up in his home safely. More importantly, this dude acts like he's feeling me! I don't have time for this shit right now."

Tiff stopped laughing. "Bitch, you are right! You don't have time for this. You have not even finished one twisted relationship. Let's not start another! Now, you focus! Are we still on for our outing sometime this week since you stood me up yesterday?"

"Yes, we can go tomorrow, Tiff. Just call me and give me a time."

"Trust me, I will call you with the time later on tonight, but I need your ass not to fall in love for at least twenty-four hours." Tiff laughed hysterically.

"Bye, Tiff!" Evea yelled, then slammed the phone down. She prepared herself to deal with Kayla when she woke up. The mother and daughter duo had so much to talk about.

*****

Adam walked through the halls with his head hung low. His hands and feet were shackled, and his eyes were sensitive to the light. The guards ushered him to his double hearing which may seal his fate. Adam reached the room with the metal door and window in the center of the door. The guards turned Adam around and removed his constraints. Inside the room, Adam was ordered to sit down in a metal chair facing the lieutenant's desk. He was then asked to swear that he would tell the truth about all the incidents he was on trial for. After Adam said his routine pledge, the lieutenant began his line of questioning.

"Adamie Artez, you are being charged with strong arm strike of a visitor and fighting with a fellow inmate with weapon. How do you plead?"

"Fight with weapon? That shit was not mine!"

The lieutenant sat up and leaned closer to Adam. "Your plea, sir?"

"Not guilty!" Adam was furious. He told his side of the story and could barely contain himself in the hearing. All of the lieutenant's words seemed like background noise. Before he knew it, the hearing was over and the lieutenant read his punishment aloud.

"Mr. Artez, in both incidents you are found guilty as charged. For your conduct in this jail, you will be transferred effective immediately. You have behaved barbaric and not only placed a court official in danger, but you placed a fellow inmate in danger, as well. You will be sent to the inner city jail, maximum security, where many of your charges are. From there, you will stand trial and be brought back to this jurisdiction to stand trial for your charges here."

Adam stood up and took all of his fate in. He did not know how to feel about what he was just told. *Maybe it will work out better in the city,* he thought. He remembered that he had more connects in the city jails than where he was, but he hated moving and getting used to new niggas and new things.

The guard stepped back into the hearing room and escorted Adam back to his cell. That would be his last night in that jail.

*****

Tiff sat on the edge of the bed wondering what was going on with her connect at the jail. She had not heard anything in a few days. She walked over to her oversized dresser to retrieve her cell phone and scrolled through it to find Steve's number.

Just when the phone began to ring, Noah slid up behind her and whispered in her ear, "Daddy's ready for some of that gushy-gushy," as he licked her neck just right.

Tiff's body became weak. She arched her back and allowed the phone to fall to her side as she ended the call. Her business would have to wait. Tiff could not resist Noah's thug loving to start her day.

*****

Kayla rolled over and cracked her eyes half opened. She now realized that last night was not a dream. She found herself in a bedroom that was not her own. Her head still pounded from all of the crying and yelling. Kayla's taste buds danced as she inhaled the wonderful smell of home cooking. The smell of Evea's brown sugar pancakes, bacon, and home fries soothed her pounding head and almost her broken heart. Kayla slowly got out of bed, being careful not to walk too hard and send sharp pains to her head. She headed for the master bathroom to get showered and find some pain medication.

Evea sang as she cooked, preparing to comfort Kayla with some home cooking as they finished their talking. She thought about Adam and felt hate creep up in her body. How could she be so stupid in love that she allowed everyone around her to get hurt and she end up alone? As she thought about everyone that was affected by her selfish actions, Evea stood at the sink with her head hung low, preparing the words for Kayla.

"Good morning, Mom."

Evea turned around, and there stood Kayla fresh with her hair pulled back in a ponytail.

"Hey, sweetie, are you hungry?"

Kayla paused. "I'm always hungry for your brown sugar pancakes!"

"Well, I have plenty of those for you," Evea said as she sat down at the table that was covered with food.

The ladies sat in silence as they enjoyed the hearty meal. Evea looked up at Kayla and stared at her as she enjoyed each bite.

"Baby, look at me." Kayla looked up with innocent eyes. "I need to come clean with you about everything. I think it is time."

Kayla put her fork down and paid close attention to her mother as Evea continued.

"Please, just listen. I am not proud of the shit that went down with your dad and me, but when he was murdered, we were on the way to working shit out. I know you are too young to understand what I'm talking about."

Kayla became agitated.

"Mom, look, I am not as naive as you think! You screwed around on Dad with Adam, and he found out. What else is it to understand? My dad died because he loved you too much!"

"Kayla, your dad died because we all made bad decisions. That's the whole truth, but I did not know Adam was the one that killed him!" Tears streamed down Evea's cheeks as she felt Kayla's pain and remembered how bad she felt that she never got to say goodbye to Té properly. "I loved your dad 'til the end. I still do! I feel so bad that I was involved with this monster that took him from me."

Kayla stood up. She was becoming more furious as her mother tried to explain everything to her. "Fuck that! I never got a choice...a choice to say if my dad would live or die. I was so young! One minute, my daddy is kissing me goodnight, and then, I don't see him no more. Was the screw worth our family? Was it, Mom?"

Evea stood with her. "Little girl, I will not stand here and be judge by you! Your daddy was a wonderful man, but he was not a saint. He was still in the streets, and on top of that, he screwed around on me one too many times! Now, I know you think he was the best thing in the world, but he was human just as I am! I protected you from his death because it was believed to be a drug transaction, and I did not want you to think of your dad like that. I was fooled by Adam, too. All these years he was protecting us from himself, and I never suspected it."

Kayla eyes became bloodshot red. "Fuck Adam!" she barked. "I hate him, and as long as my blood runs warm through my veins, he will be the enemy, and just like my daddy, I will annihilate the enemy one piece at a time. That sorry excuse for a man will pay for the destruction of my family!"

Evea stood closer to Kayla and grabbed her arms. "Look, Kay, calm your ass down and stop speaking like that! I'm sorry for everything. I love you. I hate what this has done to us."

Kayla and Evea fell to the floor as angry and painful tears battled like two rappers' metaphors in a cipher. Evea held her daughter close to her, hoping that all of her love could cure the hate inside of her.

Chapter 22

Tiff awoke singing and prancing around her room. Not the normal prissy singing most girls would do when happy. She sung Biggie's classic *Ready to Die* to herself as she prepared for her day. Noah had put it on her the night before, and she had talked to Steve from the jail concerning their business. So, all was well in her world. Tiff called Noah on the phone to be sure he knew what the plan was and where they needed to wait for the signal. Since everything was going as planned to get rid of her problem, Tiff decided she may as well call Evea to see if she was cool with their meeting time for their outing.

She pressed the speed dial number for Evea and waited for her to answer.

"Yo, chick, you up?" Tiff yelled into the phone.

"Good morning, Tiff, and yes, I'm up. I know we're meeting at ten o'clock this morning. I think I'm ready for this."

"Cool. So, get sexy, and I will see you there!"

Evea looked at the phone and asked, "What am I getting sexy for?"

"'Cause that's what you always do. Now get ya shit together, and I will meet you there."

Evea hung up and anticipated the long overdue visit.

Across town...

Adam was asleep, still not fully in tune with what the hell was going on and why he was being shipped off. That was so like Adam to never take responsibility for his actions, blaming the world for his problems.

"Inmate Adamie Artez, please step forward and place all of your belongings into this clear bag," Officer Steve demanded as he stood in Adam's cell door.

Adam stood up, looking him in the eyes. "What's going on?"

"You are being logged out for transport in a few minutes, and we need to check all of your belongings before you get in the police-transport van."

Adam obeyed his request, and then he was ushered down the corridor and through that sally port for the last time. He knew his time had come, and they wanted him out of there. With shackled hands and feet, he was taken to be checked out and await transport.

*****

Evea got up and began her morning routine. She yelled into Kayla's room to alert her that she would be ready soon. Next, she entered her walk-in closet and sat on her chaise. *What should I wear?* she thought. The weather had broken, and it was hot outside. She wouldn't complain, though, because she loved the warm weather. Evea stood on her stepladder and reached above her head to retrieve her satin one-piece Juicy Couture romper. She loved the feel and look of it.

After taking a long bath, she swept her hair to the left of her head and secured it with a jeweled hairpin, exposing her butterfly tattoo on the nape of her neck. She popped her outfit off with her hot-pink Kate Spade bag and black patent leather wedge heels.

Evea yelled for Kayla as she headed to the door, grabbing her Chanel shades on the way out. She then jumped in her black convertible BMW and prepared for her trip.

*****

Adam was on his way to his new home. He sat in the back of the patrol wagon not knowing where his life would go from there. He could hear the two officers mumbling about their day at work and all the pussy they were supposed to be getting.

He found his trip to the city a lonely one since he was the only inmate being transported. The lieutenant did not want to take any chances with Adam and another inmate fighting in the back of the transport wagon. Besides, most times, inmates from upper Pennsylvania were not transferred to the city.

Knowing he was in for a long ride, Adam let his thoughts of Evea keep him occupied. He thought back to the time when they were actually happy, before Té's death and the whole shootout thing. The thought made him smile. He wondered if Evea was thinking of him, too. He knew the type of person she was and could not believe she would leave him in jail to die.

When the wagon stopped, Adam thought something was not right. He started to get concerned when he heard both doors open. He knew he was not at the city prison yet because the time did not add up. Just when he began to yell for the guards, both doors slammed and the wagon began to move again. He took a deep breath while thinking, *Them niggas probably stopped to piss or grab something to eat with their ghetto asses.* Adam proceeded to lay back and await his arrival.

*****

Evea sang as she sped up the highway. She was trying to get her mind off of Kayla and her session the night before. She thought about how much Kayla had grown up over the years. She was also concerned about the look in her eyes and her comment about annihilating Adam. Evea wrestled with the idea that Kayla had just enough of Té in her to follow through with the threat. She was glad Adam was in jail where he belonged for more than one reason.

Evea sat up close to the dashboard to see what street she was on. She was already running late to meet Tiff due to her waiting for Kayla to get ready, which never happened. Evea's GPS announced, "Your destination is approaching on your right." She looked up and saw mature trees in various colors that lined the entrance. Then she looked at the entrance sign that had the words "Cedar Grove Meadows Cemetery" in large gold letters anchored by hand-carved gold pillars. Evea made a right and drove inside to seek the closure that she so desperately needed.

The cemetery was well-kept and had beautiful headstones on each grave. Evea had not been to the cemetery since she made the arrangements for Té's burial years prior. She drove through the grounds going five mile an hour trying to remember where Té's plot was. She followed the fancy signs that had arrows pointing to particular sections of the cemetery. She was seeking section K-22, the private burial plot with covering for shade and rain. Evea spotted what she was looking for and proceeded driving in that direction.

She knew Tiff was probably waiting on her, not pleased that she was late. Tiff hated cemeteries and usually did not attend the burial of anyone. She wanted to be there for Evea due to her circumstances, though.

Evea pulled up and parked on the side of the road behind a cherry red Lexus E-Class. She peeped over her shades and noticed a woman standing at Té's grave. "Tiff made it here early after all," she said to herself, "but when did she get this ride?"

Evea exited her car and proceeded to the grave, taking a deep breath as she walked. Upon getting a little closer to the grave, she heard a car drive up behind her. She turned around and saw a black Spider pull up and park behind her car. Evea was not sure who else would be meeting her and Tiff. As Evea stood and looked on, Tiff emerged from the sports car dressed in an all-black Chanel jumpsuit with canary yellow and black peek-a-boo toe ankle boots.

Evea turned to look toward the grave where the woman was now bending over placing items on the gravesite. Tiff waved at Evea, then turned and hurried towards the mysterious woman. Tiff yelled behind her, but Evea did not respond. When Evea made it to the grave, she was met by a beautiful woman with long, soft curls that fell over her shoulder as she laid trinkets on Té's grave. The woman stood up to acknowledge Evea's presence. As soon as they caught eyes, Evea became furious. She stood there for a minute taking in the scenery of Té's grave, which was decorated with outdoor candle holders, pictures, and a treasure box with decorative stationary. That was definitely not the woman's first time there.

"Who the fuck are YOU?!" Evea snarled. "And why are you at my husband's grave?"

Tiff finally made it to the grave and went in immediately. "Bitch, what the fuck you doing at her husband's grave? The responsibility of the jump-off usually stops after death!" Tiff stood back and looked at her closely. "Hold up. I saw you before somewhere. You were sitting in the back corner at the funeral. How can I forget that bad weave and last year's Chanel outfit you had on?! But, the question is who the fuck are you, bitch?"

Butta looked at both of them, trying to decide if she should let her furry out or just walk away.

Evea chimed in, "You standing there looking retarded like you can't speak. Well, let me help you. Get the fuck out of here, whoever you are, so I can have a proper visit with *my* husband! Oh, and don't come the fuck back."

That's when Butta let her emotions take over. "Husband?! Bitch, please! Where have you been for all of these years, huh? I've been to this grave week after week. Oh, I forgot you were busy with your other man, you whore! So, don't judge me."

Evea was beyond angry as the tears began to stream down her face. Butta's words had cut like a rusty knife. Evea lashed out, smacking Butta so hard that Butta stumbled back and dropped her purse and pictures out of her hands. Evea came with another swing. This time, the hit was a closed fist, landing right on Butta's left cheekbone. Butta was no punk, though. She swung blow for blow, scratching and smacking.

"Evea, whooooop her ass!" Tiff yelled. "Let her know where jump-offs belong!"

The women continued fighting until Butta realized they were now on top of Té's headstone. All of the trinkets were tossed about and pictures blown around. Butta fell to her knees and started to cry as she tried to pick up her pictures. Emotion overtook Evea. Here she was broken with a heavy heart, and there on Té's grave, she was defiling his memory.

Tiff ran over to Butta and kicked her in the side. Then she reached down and snatched the pictures out of her hand.

"Bitc..." Tiff stopped in mid word. There on the pictures was a child that mirrored Té. Tiff's mouth fell open. The pictures on the grave were of a little boy from infancy to a current picture of a handsome preteen in a school pose. Evea looked at Tiff and wondered what was on the pictures.

Butta yelled, coughing in between, "Bitch, give me my son's pictures!"

Evea's heart dropped to the pit of her stomach as tears covered the grave.

Tiff smacked Butta with the picture and said, "There you go, bitch. Is that how you like it?!"

Butta did not have the energy to fight back any longer. She had been fighting back for years as she raised her and Té's son alone. She found no help and no comfort in being a pregnant mistress and now a single mother.

Tiff hated that Evea was going through so much emotional turmoil. As Butta and Tiff yelled back and forth, Tiff forgot what she was really there for until she heard the sound of a vehicle coming up the paved road. The sound of the gravel mixed with dirt jogged her memory. *Shit, I was not planning on any extra company in our party,* Tiff thought to herself.

A large van approached the scene that read Sheriff

Department of Prisons on the side. All eyes were on the driver of the van. Evea had a look of shock on her face, and Tiff had a look of satisfaction. Butta wiped her face and attempted to regain the focus in her eyesight.

Adam felt the van stop and was eagerly awaiting the guards to come to the back and take him to his new home. He heard the front doors open, but he was unable to move since his hands and feet were still shackled. A few minutes went by, and Adam began to wonder what the holdup was. Finally, the silence was broken. The noise of the lock and keys jingling put Adam at ease. When the doors to the wagon swung open, Adam got the surprise of his life. There stood Corn and G dressed in all black prison outfits! It was as if Adam was seeing a ghost. When he looked at G, he saw the image of Té.

G snatched Adam from the van, dragging his shackled feet along the gravel. He punched Adam so hard that one of his teeth flew out of his mouth. Evea let out a loud scream as Tiff cheered from the sideline.

"You pussy! Only punks beat on a shackled man!" Adam yelled.

Clearly, Tiff was the mastermind who arranged to have Adam meet his fate in front of Evea and Té.

Adam continued. "E, this is what you want for me? This is how it is? All that I meant to you? And, Butta, what the fuck?"

Evea cried hysterically, "Tiff! Not like this, Tiff!" She had a moment of weakness and began to feel sorry for Adam again.

Butta was torn. She had seen all the news reports and found out that Adam was the one who had killed Té, but she never thought Evea was Adam's lover. Butta and Adam caught eyes. She could not let her brother go down like that.

"Fuck that nigga," Tiff yelled back. "He stole what both of us loved! He has to pay. He did not show Té no mercy. Fuck him, and he got my man killed!" Tiff peeped the look between Adam and Butta, not quite understanding their connection. Being about action, Tiff was not taking any chances. So, she pulled out her nine and pointed it at Butta's head just to see his reaction.

Evea let out a scream as Adam yelled, "I'm who you want! Leave her alone!"

They all turned their attention toward Tiff and Butta.

Tiff yelled, "Bitch, get on your feet!"

Adam continued to plead for Butta's life as G and Corn took the shackles off of him. G wanted to fuck him up before his demise, and he never liked to take advantage of a man because it made him feel weak. As the last lock was released, Corn went across Adam's face with a right hook. Adam swung back, and the men took turns fighting Adam, breaking him down one by one.

Butta was gripped up by Tiff and could not get loose. Tiff gestured for Butta to join Adam as she ushered her toward his bloody arena with her .9 mm. Butta knew if she did not think fast this would be her last day on earth and her son would have no parents. As she approached the bloody mess with Adam still swinging and not going down easily, G pulled out his chrome-plated custom .45 millimeter handgun and Corn pulled out his black-on-black Glock.

Evea could not look. She knew it had to be done, but was too weak to watch. So, she turned her back. Butta, now standing side by side with her brother as he kneeled with his head hung low and looking broken, feared the worse. She gained strength from the thought of her son. Butta gave Adam the look and he understood. He thought back to that day at the restaurant when he realized how gangsta Butta was.

Their signal was confirmed, and Butta swiftly elbowed Tiff in her stomach, knocking her gun to the floor. Butta spun around, ducking Tiff's blows as she pulled her .380 from her waistband and let shots rain down. Tiff dove for cover and G dumped back, hitting Butta in her shoulder. Adam grabbed Tiff's gun and returned shots as they both dove behind the prison wagon. Outnumbered and fighting for their lives, Adam and Butta remained hidden. Evea retrieved her chrome .380 from her purse and thought back to Té's instructions on shooting.

Adam was screwed up pretty bad and could not get away unless somebody died. That being his motivation, he ran from behind the wagon on one side and Butta on the other. Adam shot and was returned fire. He hit Corn in the neck as he fell down with a chest wound. Tiff and Evea, now sharing a gun, hid behind Té's tombstone.

Tiff yelled at Adam, "Nigga, you goin' down today, so don't even think about walking away from this fight. It won't happen this time!"

"Whore, please, I'm gonna kill ya last man and then take care of you two bitches!" Adam yelled back at her with fury.

G let more shots ring out, hitting Butta in the leg now. Adam returned fire, shooting him in the stomach. G stumbled backwards holding his wound and fell to the ground.

"NOOOOOOOOOOOOO!" Evea yelled.

Tiff snatched the gun from Evea and returned fire until the clip was empty. Her bullets hit the prison wagon, and she landed one in Adam's leg. Adam heard the last bullet in the clip and came from behind the wagon limping and breathing shallow from his chest wound. While approaching Evea and Tiff, he ordered them from behind the tombstone.

"Showtime, bitches!"

Evea came out first and then Tiff. Adam ordered Butta to keep the gun and an eye pointed at Tiff.

Butta approached Tiff and smacked her across her face with her gun. "Bitch, that's for earlier!"

Adam focused his attention on Evea. They stood face to face with Té's tombstone as the backdrop. "How could you do this to me?!" he began. "All these years, were they a lie? You stole all of my money and attempted to have me killed! So, I guess our life together did not mean anything!" Adam yelled, placing the gun under Evea's chin. "Look at me!"

When Evea looked up, she spit in his face. "Fuck you! I loved you even when I shouldn't have. I risked my whole life for you, and you repay me with lies? Keeping me away from my friends and family all of these years for your own selfish gain! My life was turned INSIDE OUT, and I lost it all because of you!"

Adam slapped Evea in the face. Her truth was too much for him. He wanted her to pay for putting him back in prison and stealing his money, but the love he felt for Evea made it hard to pull the trigger. Butta and Tiff stood idle as their life played out like a soap opera.

As Butta learned more about her brother and Evea's relationship, she let her attention float away from Tiff. She tried to gain Adam's attention.

"Adam, stay focused. We have bodies lying on the ground, and we have to get out of here. The whole police force will be looking for you soon."

Tiff took advantage of her opportunity. She kicked Butta in the stomach and took off running toward her car. Tiff knew if she made it to her car, she would be able to get enough heat to take out a small country. Butta struggled to catch Tiff. Due to her wounds, she attempted to shoot while running. Tiff made it close to the street, while Butta continued shooting. She ran for cover behind her car, and Butta followed! Butta ran in the street and had Tiff cornered, gun to head.

"Look, bitch, I'm not moving another inch! Stand the fuck up!" Butta stepped back to allow Tiff to stand up.

Hearing a car approaching, they both looked up. Butta lowered her weapon and appeared to relax. *Boom!* Butta was struck head-on by a powder pink BMW. She flew up in the air and fell back to the ground. Her body lay lifeless in the road.

Tiff could not imagine who just saved her life. She entered

her car to retrieve her weapons, and when she emerged with weapons drawn, she noticed the car door open and Butta's weapon gone.

*****

Several feet away, Evea was about to meet her maker at the hands of a man she shared love and a bed with. Adam had no reason to leave Evea alive. Things were too screwed up and would never be the same. Evea refused to go out without dignity, though. She stood up eye to eye with Adam, her chin up, and ready to meet her husband on the other side if need be.

"You call yourself a man; you call what we had love? Well, that's a joke. The connection I thought I had with you must have not been too strong. You murdered my husband out of fear that I would never be fully yours. You disgust me! I hate you. I hate the things that represent you!"

Adam stood there with tears streaming down his face, hating how vulnerable he was for Evea. He knew only one thing would bring closure to the entire situation.

"You ungrateful bitch! I loved you so much that I would have died for you, and you turn around and fuck my homie and steal all of my money! Everything I did was for you...fuck! I hate this, but, Evea, it is over."

Adam cocked his gun back and pointed it straight at Evea's head. She embraced her fate and clinched down as she stood on Té's grave. For the first time, she took responsibility for her part in cheating on Té and ushering her lover turned enemy into their world. She closed her eyes and said her last prayer.

Bang! Bang! Bang! Evea's body jerked back and forth. She opened her eyes, feeling her torso for blood, but her romper was dry.

She looked at Adam, who was holding his chest with blood dripping on his hands. He fell to the ground, and Evea's eyes widened as she looked at his shooter. In shock, Evea fell to the ground sobbing.

Kayla stood over Adam and screamed, "You lowdown nothing excuse of a man! Fuck you! This is for my daddy!"

Bang! Bang! Two shots at point blank range in between his eyes sent Adam straight to hell.

Tiff approached the scene and took over. She sent Kayla away as she consoled Evea once again. Then Tiff made her phone call so Ramir, Love, Noah, and Jay-Roc could come for the cleanup, while Tiff sat in the car as Evea had her time with Té.

NOTE FROM THE AUTHOR

Lai`a D. Johnson MS

I would like to say thank you for taking this journey with me. I had a wonderful time spinning this tale. Evea was a woman that allowed her weakness to destroy her life. There is a little bit of Evea in us all. Taking chances without thinking and testing the limits come with a price. Are you willing to lose everything to live in the moment and throw caution to the wind? I'm sure some of you said yes, but next time you find yourself faced with a moral dilemma, think twice, because you may get turned INSIDE OUT! See you all next time between the pages.

LJ

BLUE MIRAGE SNEAK PEEK
COMING SOON...

INTRO...10/5/06

Shanna awoke to the sound of rain hitting her window. She thought about what her day would bring. She had so much to sort out and so much to do. While shuffling things around on her desk, she stumbled across a big envelope that she had been putting off for a few days. She reluctantly opened it, and its contents were nothing short of disturbing. Her eyes grew wide and her stomach churned. Everything that had happened to Shanna up to this point all returned to her mind as she franticly searched through the unmarked package. Shanna scrambled through her desk to find a pen. She had to document the package's arrival in her journal...

Time: 5:30 p.m.
Place: Home office; sitting at the window
Mood: SHOCKED
I will start by saying this is a very complicated story to tell. I have never been so confused in my life about the roles that authority figures play in the place where I work. I am relieved to write this, but at the same time, I feel a profound sense of sadness and disappointment. The people involved in

my story are deceitful, and they need to pay for their actions. The past year of my life has been nothing short of colorful. They create a mirage that fools all that they come in contact with: **A mirage, by definition, is an optical illusion caused by an atmospheric condition.** That is exactly what happened in this situation. Beware, you will hear some things that will shock you, but pay close attention so as not to get caught up in THE BLUE MIRAGE.

(Accompanying this journal entry are pictures, audiotapes, and a manuscript to support this story.)

Signed,

S.B.

IT ALL STARTED WHEN...

The day seemed to be going well for Diashana Butler, known as Shanna for short. The sun was shining, and she felt well rested since her midnight escapade with the love of her life, Tristen Stevens. Diashana was a thirty-two-year-old female who had done all right for herself. She held a position as the Director of Inmate Programs at Pinckney Peabody Correctional Facility in Philadelphia, Pennsylvania.

Diashana was a sensual looking female. She pulled that off without trying. She always looked as if she was seducing any man in her view. That was a problem for her, though, because it caused many women she met to hold on tight to their men. She had a medium build and hips perfectly proportioned with her ass and thighs. Her face was smooth as milk chocolate and the home of two chestnut brown eyes with long, jet-black lashes that she fluttered regularly.

Diashana entered the prison and walked straight to the sign-in desk as she did for the past five years. The ritual was familiar, but not this particular morning. As the last letter of her name hit the page, she felt a swift gust of wind. She looked up and could not believe her eyes.

Surrounded by men and women with all black uniforms on, she was escorted to the captain's office. The fifty-foot walk seemed like ten miles. Shanna's breathing began to quicken, and she could feel her blood thicken in her veins. She questioned the officer's reason for the dramatic entrance. None of the glorified correctional officers spoke a word.

Once she was placed in the office, the lieutenant appeared seeming agitated. Without introduction, he ordered her to tell them who she was bringing drugs in for. Shanna was definitely no angel but far from a drug pusher. She attempted to wake up from this nightmare, but to no avail. The lieutenant's stinky breath and loud screams confirmed that she was definitely awake. He spouted names at her while giving her the angriest snarl she had ever seen.

Finally, Shanna got her thoughts together and said, "What the hell are you talking about? I want to see my lawyer!"

The Captain smiled and replied, "This is the PPS, and in here, you do what you are told! And right now, you're going to get strip searched along with your locker and your vehicle as stated in the PPS search policy under section (a)1234."

Shanna reared back in her seat and looked at the captain,

lieutenant, and his burly wide-eyed female sergeant.

"Who the hell do you think you're fucking with!?" she yelled.

"If you have nothing to hide, then we wouldn't be having this conversation!" the captain replied. "Now, follow the sergeant's orders and drop 'em. I'll be outside!"

Captain John Stern was a tall white man in his mid forties, one of the few Anglo-Saxons left that thought he was pure bred. So, the thought of an educated black was almost impossible to him, which explained why he chose to go into corrections. The straightforward follow-the-orders mentality and a chain of command suited him. He got off on the power, especially the power over women and other minorities. His drawers were in a bunch ever since his new warden's first day and his old academy buddy's departure. Captain Stern made it up the ranks, kicking ass all the way. He did not care who he hurt in the process as long as he was glorified in the end. His new boss was black *and* female, which made her twice as repulsive. The idea that she fucked her way to the top bugged him even more.

Shanna sat back in the hard wooden chair that reminded her of her grade school days. She started to think back to several events in the prison. As she rolled her cortex, she tried to recall a series of events that may have led up to that point in her life. Her life flashed before her like a movie in slow motion. She could smell the pungent aroma of the K-9 unit, which further confirmed it was her reality. She escaped from her body and became numb. All activity around her was nothing but background noise. As she sat there with tears flowing like rushing water in the Caribbean, it all made sense...

Chapter 2

The halls were packed for miles, and you only saw men in brown jumpsuits. They came in all different hues and sizes. Shanna made her way through the crowd. There were four officers running the inmates to the gym and to afternoon activities at Peabody Corrections. Shanna entered the activity room and, as usual, the room was not set up for her creative writing class. The chairs were stacked on top of each other, and the room smelled like hot, sweaty ass. There were no supplies for the day's lesson, and there was no officer willing to assist her with bringing the inmates to the class.

That was nothing new to deal with in the prison system. Most people that worked there hated their job or were too lazy to actually do their job. The other group hated the inmates and treated them all like shit on a stick. Not Shanna, though. She was compassionate and treated them like human beings. She never in a million years thought that such animals would employ her. Her career path was law, but she never pursued it after she lost the state finals mock trial in high school. After her lost and the lost her debate team endured, she felt unworthy of practicing law.

Shanna began to get the classroom set up. The room was a blah cream color with cement walls. A large window was on the left wall of the room to allow for some visibility of the outside world.

The inmates came streaming into the room, laughing and playing amongst each other like children. Shanna had a pretty straight-to-the-point personality and said whatever she felt.

"Come into my classroom and stop acting like confused puppies fresh out the womb!"

They just stared at her. They were used to her abrasive comments; they knew she meant nothing by them.

A voice yelled over all the noise in the room, "Ms. Butler, did you miss me?"

"Yeah, I missed you like I miss cramps!" she replied, as the entire class laughed out loud.

"Damn, Ms. B! You must be in your bag today."

"Nigga, I'm in my bag, and I'm about to put you in it, too, if you don't shut the hell up and let me start the damn class!"

More of the back and forth joking and word play went on throughout the remainder of the class. Despite the horseplay, Shanna actually reached some of the inmates and had them thinking about writing when they were released.

Shanna could see the lieutenant's office from her classroom. He was not fond of the staff talking with respect to the inmates. He had a suspicious nature that came from him working in internal affairs for fifteen years. LT. Grenich was a medium built Caucasian man that looked to be in his early forties, but he was really in his fifties. He had a few secrets of his own.

His major secret was that he craved the Brown Sugar like a sweet's addiction.

He was always staring at Shanna's plump ass each time she walked by him. That day was no different. Shanna wore a black blazer and some True Religion stretch jeans that grabbed her body at each curve. The LT was eyeing her the entire morning, but not for the reasons Shanna believed. The LT got off on watching her and fantasized about how soft her body would feel against his often, but today was business.

The LT's phone rang.

"LT Grenich here!"

A female's voice on the other end greeted him. "Are you free to talk?"

"Who is this?"

"You know I don't tell my name on the phone. I just need to know are you working on that project."

"Yes, it is under surveillance right now. I won't know anything for a few days. I will call you then."

The class was over, and Shanna appeared in the LT's door. Startled, he looked up and abruptly hung up the phone.

"May I help you with something, Ms. Butler?"

"Sure, you can lock the room back up. I'm on my way out."

He sat there and looked straight through her. "Okay, I will handle it," he said with some hesitation.

Then he watched Shanna walk away as he drooled like a newborn baby on the tit.

Shanna walked towards the exit down a long, cold

hallway. Inmates stared and whispered as she brought them to fireballs of lust. Shanna acted as if she did not notice their lustful stares. This was her way of getting through the day without snapping. After making it to the exit, she realized she had left her car keys in her office. She sighed and thought to herself, *I have to pass all these horny-ass niggas again.* With no other choice, she turned around and walked the plank again.

Shanna arrived at her office, grabbed her keys, and was on her way back out, when one of her students appeared at the door. Peter Saxon was an inmate that she spoke to a lot. He was truly gangsta or a "boss" as some called him on the street. He was well known in the prison and feared by many guards and inmates alike. Pete, or P for short, was not an aggressive inmate on the surface, but he could have anyone touched from the jail to the streets with one word. This type of power frightened the warden and all of Shanna's counterparts.

P stood five-feet ten-inches and was nice to look at. He was blessed with the silkiest black hair imaginable. His waves spun like a raging sea. If one looked at his hair too long, they easily got seasick. He always was crisp - even in prison browns he had to be sharp. He recognized his power and walked in it on a regular basis. The talk of the jail was his latest act of defiance. He adorned his feet with the latest model of Louis Vuitton running shoes. This was what he called "BOSS SHIT." That act of defiance made top story on "prison news" due to the heaviness of the move. P liked when others recognized his G or respected his hand, as he often said. Him sporting Louis in the prison was heavy on so many different levels. He had to have a guard or someone on payroll, and that was not cheap to do.

P entered the office and began to hold general conversation. Knowing where the conversation was headed, Shanna tried to hurry him along. He had been trying to get at her for a long time, but she was not indulging him. It wasn't because she was not feeling him, but because she knew where their relationship would take her in the long run. Despite his failed advances, she and P remained cool.

"Where are you about to go, Ms. Butler?"

"I don't think I have to report to you," Shanna replied with a straight-up look. "Mr. P, last time I checked, I don't have a wedding ring on."

"No, you don't," he replied. "But you know that engagement ring is only temporary. I'm just letting him borrow you until I get out!"

They both laughed.

"Real shit, though. I just need to talk to you, and I wanted to see how you were doing."

"I'm doing fine, but I'm sure that's not why you're here." She looked up right into his eyes. "I know KM told you I was here after he left my class."

KM, or Kevin Miller, was an inmate in her class. She took extra time to help him with his project, which he had to complete before he got parole.

"Now that we got the bullshit out of the way," P said, "when you gonna be mine and let me hit that big ass? You know I get what I want."

Shanna's face displayed the image of shock and disbelief. "I think it's time for you to go now."

"We both are grown," P replied. "Why yo' looking like you don't know you got a big ass?"

"Goodbye, Peter."

P stood up and left out of the office. Shanna may have sent him away, but his presence lingered long after his exit. She walked away tingling all over.

www.ingramcontent.com/pod-product-compliance
Lightning Source LLC
Chambersburg PA
CBHW032043240626
47154CB00003B/1058